Edward O. Phillips

# *A Month of Sundays*

A Novel

*Cormorant Books*

The publisher gratefully acknowledges the support of the Canada Council for the Arts
and the Ontario Arts Council for its publishing program. We acknowledge the financial
support of the Government of Canada through the Canada Book Fund (CBF) for
our publishing activities, and the Government of Ontario through the Ontario Media
Development Corporation, an agency of the Ontario Ministry of Culture,
and the Ontario Book Publishing Tax Credit Program.

LIBRARY AND ARCHIVES CANADA CATALOGUING IN PUBLICATION

Phillips, Edward, 1931–
A month of Sundays / Edward O. Phillips.

"A Geoffry Chadwick novel".
Issued also in electronic formats.
ISBN 978-1-77086-211-1

1. Title.

PS8581.H567M56 2012     C813'.54     C2012-903496-7

Cover photograph and design: Angel Guerra / Archetype
Interior text design: Tannice Goddard, Soul Oasis Networking
Printer: Trigraphik LBF

Printed and bound in Canada.

The interior of this book is printed on 100% post-consumer waste recycled paper.

CORMORANT BOOKS INC.
390 Steelcase Road East, Markham, Ontario, L3R 1G2
www.cormorantbooks.com

*For Susan and Kenneth*

Now is the winter of our discontent
Made glorious summer by this son of York.

SHAKESPEARE: *RICHARD III*

# 1

*T* have always detested funerals. Granted, this observation does not brand me as unusual. Most people when faced with a list of drab duties they must on occasion perform would put funerals near the bottom. Small wonder. Most burial services are hastily slung together affairs, conceived in haste after a person has died and all too often left to the unctuous discretion of the funeral home.

To begin with, a funeral home is not a home but a business, with accounts receivable, a price list, and bottom lines. A funeral parlour is not a parlour but a large rectangular room with a coffin, preferably closed, at one end and a scattering of straight-backed chairs for those either too feeble or too overcome to stand. Curtains are drawn, lighting subdued, carpets deep piled. It would seem to me that if ever you were not to be disturbed by voices pitched at normal level that time is when you are dead, but such is the custom of the country that once through the door of a funeral establishment the visitors lower their voices to near inaudibility.

I speak only of the pre-funeral visitation, two sessions: four to six and seven to nine, allowing the bereaved one hour for a sandwich and coffee. The visitation itself is not unlike a cocktail party, but without the cocktails. After greeting the family with obligatory hugs, followed by clasped hands and sincere eye-locks meant to convey caring, the guests stand around talking about nothing in particular. The only taboo topic appears to be the body in the coffin, almost as if the central figure in this ephemeral drama is no more than part of the furnishings, like the standing lamps with parchment shades or the gilt framed painting of Sunset in the Rockies.

All this is prelude to the funeral itself, a pastiche of indifferent organ playing, hymns pitched a tone too high for the hardy few who attempt to sing, and a eulogy by numbers from a minister who did not know the deceased, or dead person. "O death, where is thy sting? O grave, where is thy victory?" while the mourners wonder about how soon they can get back to the office, or whether there will be anything to eat after the service.

If I appear jaundiced about funerals, the reason is that I am. I recently buried my wife of only five years. Furthermore, I just turned seventy, not one of the jollier milestones of a lifetime. In spite of the smiley-face slogan that "Eighty is the new seventy," I am still acutely aware of the ineluctable fact that the major portion of my life has been lived. Way too old to be high-hearted, I nevertheless married for love and the reassuring realization that I would have a wonderful companion for my declining years.

I turned out to be half right. Elinor proved to be the ideal wife for an elderly, crotchety, and — according to most — terminal bachelor. In truth, I was a widower, my first wife having died young in an accident. I have not had very good luck with wives. A runaway truck killed the first, breast cancer the second. I will not dwell on the details about Elinor. There is a pornography of illness which I refuse to countenance. Simply mention that a person is ill, be it cancer or heart problems or AIDS, and someone within earshot will want to learn all the particulars. What are the symptoms, the treatment, the length of stay in hospital? Will there be surgery? How many stitches? How long has the patient been given to live? No doubt for some this relentless cross-examination is meant to indicate concern, but there remains an element of prurience, a barely repressed relish over clinical details.

While Elinor lay dying I refused to play the game. Fortunately I did not have to. When I married Elinor I acquired two stepchildren, Jane and Gregory, along with assorted grandchildren. Gregory, his wife Laura, and their children live in Toronto, an arrangement that suits me fine. I have low tolerance for small children, and Gregory and Laura believe their children walk on water. Childish whims are endlessly indulged, the children eat with the grownups, and the word "no" is all too infrequently heard. Elinor used to visit her son in Toronto, leaving me happily behind in Westmount. When we married I made clear I was not saying "I do" to her entire family, nor she to mine. Elinor's daughter Jane has turned out to be a throwback to an earlier century. Her children stand when an adult enters the room; "please" and "thank you" are much in evidence; bedtimes are non-negotiable. Jane has turned out to be a conventional woman at a time when testing the limits of acceptable behaviour often seems the norm. She tolerates telemarketers and thanks recorded messages. She is very hard work, but she rushed in to fill the vacuum left by her mother's illness and death, and insisted on taking charge of funeral arrangements.

I had wanted a private burial service for Elinor, to be followed by a bang-up memorial service with professional musicians, a well rehearsed choir, and eulogies delivered by old and close friends. Jane, however, wanted the service to be held with the coffin present. I thought of pulling age and rank, but reconsidered. Jane had known Elinor a lot longer than I, and in terms of the Grand Design did the form of the obsequies really matter? The price of my capitulation was to have the coffin closed for the visitation. I wanted Elinor to be remembered vibrant and alive, not made up with pale orange foundation and wearing her best black dress. Jane hesitated. Wouldn't her mother's friends want one last look?

It was then that I brought the flat of my hand down on the table so hard it hurt. This condition was not open to discussion.

4

I did not want the service held in the undertaker's dreary little chapel. I did not want the goddamned visitation. And I was as sure as bloody hell that my late wife was not going to be on display in her coffin like something in a counterculture art gallery. Jane took the point, compressed her already thin lips (she takes after her father), and agreed the casket would remain closed.

My outburst has resulted in a coolness between Jane and me; I confess I have made no move to heal the breach. Jane is a pain in the ass, and now that Elinor is dead I no longer have to make nice with my stepdaughter.

The service went off as I expected. The coffin lay on a dolly in front of the chapel. I suppose as coffins go it was handsome, oak with antiqued gold handles. I chose it, I paid for it. On top was a wreath of gardenias, Elinor's favourite flower, again from me. Two wreaths of white roses flanked the coffin, from Jane and Gregory. We had requested that instead of flowers donations be made to the cancer society. The flowers were the best part of the service.

As mourners filed in, the organist — a woman in her sixties — played Bach badly, many missed notes and a fluctuating dynamic level. Her suspiciously shiny auburn hair had the look of being patted but never combed, and her black academic gown needed pressing. The ad hoc minister, ecumenical and also unpressed, delivered the usual platitudes and homilies: a rich full life sadly terminated; sorely missed by family and friends; an influence for good that will linger. Let us pray. We stood to sing a hymn. I never sing hymns, mainly because I am seldom in church; but the slack was taken up by an enthusiastic baritone who sang out-of-tune and a mezzo who sang slightly off the beat. The service ended with an invitation into the parlour for refreshments.

The immediate family followed the hearse to the crematorium. I had managed to get through the service fairly well, as I had done my real grieving when Elinor went into the hospital and I knew she was not coming out. As the illness progressed she moved further and further away from me until she came to a place where I could no longer reach her. Her death came as a relief. By then I had reached a point of exhaustion unlike any I had experienced. I could have shovelled snow, planted a garden, climbed a mountain; but my mind felt numb. I could not even argue with Jane about the form of the service, with the exception of the closed coffin, no more than Elinor herself would have wanted.

I had thought the worst was over, but I was wrong. When, after a brief prayer to which I did not listen, I watched the coffin slide down a ramp into the furnace I felt that I might faint, or double up, or cry out. But I didn't. I endured the terrible finality, took several deep breaths, and left. I did not weep. Tears seemed too easy an outlet, and Elinor would have frowned on a public display of grief.

During the service in the funeral chapel, as I deliberately tuned out on the eulogy, I had a sudden, illuminating idea. More than a mere idea, it seemed a flash of inspiration. I was going to throw a party and invite all of Elinor's friends to celebrate her life. Instead of a solemn and sombre memorial service I would hold a wake, well perhaps not a wake as by then Elinor will have been buried beside her parents in the Mount Royal Cemetery. There would be a party, a wonderful party, the kind where the women cry and then get drunk, while the men get drunk and then cry. Elinor deserved better, far better than this shabby service whose only redeeming feature was the large attendance. Elinor obviously had more friends than I had realized. I doubt my own funeral will be so well attended.

The more I thought about the party, the better I liked the idea. During the ride from the crematorium back to the undertaker's I was already planning the event. The prospect of organizing the celebration for Elinor even helped me to endure my sister Mildred, who had come down from Toronto for the funeral. Mildred is the kind of woman whose behaviour at funerals makes staying alive seem an excellent option. Like many women of a certain age, Mildred gets off on grief. Nothing cheers her up like a good funeral, and how much more when the dead person is family.

Mildred was the only member of my immediate family to be present at the ceremony; my father has been long dead and my mother is too old and frail to attend. As a result we were the only passengers in the limousine heading back to the undertaker's.

"I won't talk, Geoffry," she began once the car was in motion. "I know you'll want to think about poor dear Elinor. It was a lovely service, wasn't it."

"It was a shitty service, Mildred, and you know it. Anybody who attends as many funerals as you do has to have developed some yardstick of quality."

"Geoffry Chadwick, how can you say such a thing!" Mildred sat up straight to indicate disapproval. I am certain one of the reasons she enjoys funerals is that, like many women of her age, she looks good in black. "You know," she reached out a gloved hand to clasp mine, "you mustn't let your loss make you bitter."

"I did not lose Elinor, Mildred. She died." Mildred removed her hand. "And why are you wearing gloves? We're having the warmest Indian Summer in memory."

As I listened to her saying something about respect for the dead, I could not suppress a little frisson of pleasurable malice. Mildred has ugly hands, hence the gloves. *Voilà tout.* She even wears gloves to go shopping. They regularly snag on her engagement ring; but, as any rich hairdresser knows, vanity is right up there beside hunger and sex as a force that drives civilization.

By the time we returned from the crematorium most of the guests had left, but not before making heavy inroads into the refreshments. In order to give this unfortunate funeral event a semblance of shape, I took Mildred, along with Jane, Gregory, and their partners, to my club for lunch. By asking Mildred to be my hostess I made certain she would carry the conversation, leaving me free to concentrate on my three pre-lunch, straight-up, dry martinis. I knew I would be sorry this evening; but I was not about to toast my late wife in sherry or vodka and tonic. I couldn't remember the last time I drank three martinis, nor did I particularly want to.

After lunch, the two pairs of parents excused themselves as they had to get back to Elinor's house, where Gregory and his family were staying, to rescue the baby sitter. Knowing the children involved, I would have been tempted to hire a security guard instead of an unsuspecting sitter, but the decision was not mine to make. Besides, another problem had presented itself, that of my sister. Having come straight from the airport to the undertaker's, Mildred now wanted to visit Mother at Maple Grove Manor, where she currently lived. Mother is old and frail, her grasp of reality tenuous. One of the best things that ever happened to Mother was Elinor, who proved adept at handling her. In effect, Elinor dealt with Mother by not dealing with her. Elinor's own mother used to get around town on her broomstick, until old age, inflexible values, and terminal probity did her in. Elinor found my mother — vague, alcoholic, unthreatening, and non-judgemental — easy to be around. They became friends at once.

The upshot was that I had not yet told Mother about Elinor's death. I knew she would take it hard, and I wanted to present Mother with a *fait accompli* so she would not feel obliged to attend the funeral. I am the first to admit I was thinking of myself as much as of Mother. Getting through the funeral service and subsequent cremation was going to be enough of a trial without wondering whether Mother was going to disintegrate during the service. Now I was painted into a corner. How to explain

Mildred, head to toe in black including stockings, appearing suddenly in Mother's room at Maple Grove. Mildred, who has all the innate tact of a Florida alligator, would blurt out the news about the funeral, to Mother's immense distress.

Obviously, I would have to accompany Mildred to Maple Grove, oblige her to wait in the lobby, and go upstairs to break the news to Mother. Fortunately, I experienced the false courage that three martinis and a good beaujolais can foster. Not surprisingly Mildred registered astonishment bordering on shock that Mother did not know of Elinor's — passing.

"Death," I corrected.

"But, Geoffry, how could you possibly not have told Mother? Doesn't she have every right to know?"

"Yes, she does. But I wanted to choose the most appropriate time. I know bad news travels fast. The internet could learn a thing or two about speedy transmission when it comes to word of a nice death. Now, this is what we will do. You will wait in the lobby of the residence. I will go up and break the news to Mother in the best way I can. Then, as a diversion, I will announce you are here, and call down to the front desk to send you up. Your unanticipated presence will take her mind off the bad news. And you will knock yourself out to be diverting. *C'est bien compris?*"

"Don't you think I had better be there, for moral support?"

I understood Mildred hated the thought of not being present for the delivery of bad news, reality TV without the intervening screen. But I was in no mood to indulge her.

"The second the two of us walk into the room, you dressed in black like the Three Fates, she will know something is up. Mother may be wafty, but she is not a complete idiot."

Mildred thought for a minute. "Well, perhaps you are right."

"I'm glad you agree. I'll have the hall porter call us a cab."

&

Now that Mother has her evening meal at five-thirty in the afternoon, she has her first drink at four, while the other residents are having their tea. Imagine dinner at half past five with the evening yawning ahead, one of the many terrors besetting those who cling to life. Since it was shortly after four when Mildred and I pulled up outside Maple Grove Manor, Mother had already poured her first drink. (I have a private paid arrangement with the nurse who buys vodka for Mother to dilute it with water in the bottle. With vodka who can tell, and Mother is then able to make it down to the dining room for dinner.)

"Well, Geoffry, I didn't expect you today of all days. Pour yourself a drink, dear."

I complied. Lukewarm watered vodka is not my idea of a good time, but my martinis had begun to let me down.

"Why do you say, 'Today of all days,' Mother?"

"Well, you did have the funeral to attend."

"Funeral?"

"Elinor's funeral, dear. Have you forgotten?"

"As a matter of fact, no. But how did you come to find out?"

"The Director saw the death notice in the paper and came

to see me. I didn't mention it to you as I knew you would tell me in your own good time."

I sat in one of the wing chairs I had brought from Mother's apartment. "I wanted to tell you after the funeral. But I should have known that bad news travels at the speed of light. Well, it's done."

We sat silent. Mother can still surprise me, which I suppose is another way of saying she harks back to an era of civility that is fast disappearing. This civility, of the sort I remembered as a child, is thin on the ground these days. Perhaps the civilized man is going the way of other endangered species, the snail darter and the Siberian tiger. I was certainly well brought up, according to the standards of my youth. To stand whenever an older person enters a room is so ingrained that I have stood when that older person turned out to be some years my junior. Likewise, when a lady joins or leaves a table I struggle to my feet, no easy task when the chair has no arms and the table is not solidly anchored.

A gentleman, or a lady, attempts to put others at ease, never placing himself (*pace*, ladies) front and centre. He never takes the first canapé, nor the last, confident that more food will appear. He knows who he is and does not chase after the spotlight. The current locution "in your face" would be anathema to the true gentleman. Mother taught me manners with a combination of example and gentle but firm insistence: thank-you notes rewritten until legible, helping ladies and older men on and off with coats, never to interrupt when someone else — even of one's own age — was speaking, denying oneself the last piece of cake or pie until pressed by the hostess, and sprinkling "Please, Thank you, You're welcome" liberally, like confetti at a wedding.

I have observed that gay men are perhaps the last bastion of what many consider to be an outdated and quaint civility. Lesbians are hopeless: a bottle of whiskey and a toothbrush glass on the bare table and help yourself. Pizza served in the delivery box. You take the folding bridge chair; I'll sit on the packing crate. Cats on the comfortable chairs and not to be disturbed. But gay men, under the camp chatter and manu-factured malice, often demonstrate genuine and uncomplicated kindness, doing the right thing and making even disaster into a huge joke.

Mother harks back to an earlier century. Even with her unmistakeably Canadian accent she would have been right at home in the antebellum South, more Melanie than Scarlett I grant you; but she would never have acknowledged that the North had won the war.

Mother reached for her tumbler and took a long, meditative swallow.

"I hope you are going to do something nice in Elinor's memory, perhaps flowers each year at the church as a memorial, maybe a donation to charity."

"Flowers do seem like a good idea. But I'm thinking about having a party for Elinor, a kind of celebration of her life — with all her friends."

"That sounds like a good idea. People always enjoy a good party. Poor Elinor. Now she is at rest. After all, life with you couldn't have been easy."

"Why the vote of confidence, Mother?"

"Goodness me, Geoffry, you were already set in your ways before you turned twenty-one."

About to retort that a preference for regular meal times and neatly pressed shirts did not brand me as a crank, I changed the subject.

"Has that dotty old fool Barlowe been annoying you?" My reference was to the resident bore who liked to buttonhole people in the lobby and tell off-colour jokes.

"Not as much. He always expects me to laugh, and I never do. Why, just the other day he told me a pointless story about two nuns who were riding their bicycles through an old part of Paris. One nun reportedly said to the other, 'You know, I've never come this way before.' Her companion replied, 'It must be the cobblestones.' At this point Mr. Barlowe began to wheeze; I thought he might be having an attack. But no, he was just laughing. I told him I didn't realize that nuns were allowed out on bicycles, but what better way to sightsee in an old city like Paris. He shook his head and went away. A tiresome man, but harmless."

Before I could comment, the door burst open and Mildred plunged into the room.

"Geoffry, I thought you were going to call me. Hello, Mother." Mildred kissed the older woman on both cheeks. "I suppose Geoffry has told you the sad news?"

If she had been hoping for a good weep-in, where she could play the role of compassionate daughter comforting the grieving mother, she was to be sorely disappointed.

"Why do you say that, Mildred?" Mother sat up straight. "Elinor was ill, very ill. Her death came as a release. Just as mine will do one of these days."

Mother took a hefty swallow of her drink and deflated into her chair. I understood then that Mother had reached a point in her life when death, any death, no longer touched her very deeply. I could almost have envied her tranquility. Not even the prospect of her own exit managed to dismay.

I stood. "I think I'll move along. Mildred, you can have a visit with Mother before she goes down to dinner." I have trouble saying the word "supper" for the main meal of the day.

I made my escape. Mildred was staying with an old school friend, so I did not have to cope with her this evening, a minor blessing. The events of the day had ground me down. What I needed, almost more than air to breathe, was the restorative balm of solitude. As it was now too late for a nap, I planned to go home and get quietly drunk. Tomorrow I must pay the price, but at the moment tomorrow seemed days away.

As I rode the elevator down to the lobby, I remembered when Mildred and I were children Mother used to complain that summer weeks spent at the country cottage were a month of Sundays. Mildred and I used to laugh because Sunday to us meant no school. Now that Elinor is dead every days seems a cold, wet Sunday. More than just a month, I faced a lifetime of Sundays, with every seventh day a double-barrelled threat. The prospect did not please, but time has a way of dribbling past. With the help of scotch, the Sunday *Times* and preparations for the party I knew I would scrape through. What other choice did I have?

## 2

*A* hangover at seventy is not like a hangover at forty, fifty, or even sixty. It is a major affliction. Yet in a curious kind of way, my fragile condition on the day following the funeral turned out to be a bonus. So focused was I on the ache in my head and the discomfort in my gut that I had little awareness left over to brood on the fact that I was well and truly alone. I showered, pulled on some clothes, and went to a nearby eatery for a high-calorie, artery-clogging breakfast of eggs, bacon, sausage, pancakes, hash browns, toast, and several cups of coffee. So much unaccustomed food in the morning tends to stun, and it was in a state of blunted awareness that I strolled through the beautiful October day to the house Elinor and I had shared.

Ours had not been a conventional marriage. When a man in his sixties, who has lived most of his adult life as a homosexual, marries a widow some years his junior, attention is usually paid. To be sure, a gay man in a pin-striped suit does not attract the attention of one who bleaches his hair and wears a gold ring through his eyebrow. Like forest creatures scrutinized on nature programs, I have always tried to blend in with my surroundings. My sartorial requirements do not extend to tattoos, construction boots, and artificially shredded jeans.

Another uncommon feature of our marriage was that Elinor and I maintained separate establishments. This possibly unconventional arrangement sprang less from lack of commitment than simple inertia. When we met, I was living in a comfortable apartment in a well maintained building no more than a pleasant walk to the small townhouse where Elinor had chosen to settle. She had managed to make the house comfortable without gutting it first. Her efficient kitchen did not resemble an operating theatre; her bathrooms did not aspire to be spas; and walls designed by the architect remained securely in place. From her first marriage had come silver and china; from her mother's house some choice antiques; from her own past the bits and pieces accumulated over the span of a lifetime.

My condominium apartment had a similar history: silver and china from an early marriage, some choice pieces from my mother's house when it was dismantled, and my own accumulation of books, records, pictures, and what the young today call "stuff." Once we had married, we faced the idea of amalgamation. Yet even with ruthless determination to unload all non-essentials, we realized that between us there were simply too many possessions to be absorbed into her house, while to relocate to my apartment was obviously not an option.

The logical solution would have been to buy a larger house. But after years of carefree condo living, I did not want to undertake a furnace with a service contract; a roof that needed an annual checkup, not unlike the owner; a garden to be weeded; snow to be shovelled; leaves raked. The prospect of painters, plumbers, carpenters tramping in to bring the new property up to our specifications defeated me. I had no wish, at this point in my life, to shoulder the responsibility of a house: burglar alarms, smoke detectors, insurance policies, friendly neighbours, carpenter ants burrowing in the deck, and squirrels nesting in the soffits. Nor, I have to admit, was Elinor overjoyed at the prospect of uprooting herself one more time. Why tamper with the status quo?

The more we examined our options, the better we liked the way we were. As things worked out, I spent most of my time at Elinor's house. On occasion, for no good reason, which is the best reason of all, we would go to my apartment with a couple of videos and send out for chicken or pizza. We felt as though we were not married and borrowing a friend's apartment for a tryst. The evening usually ended with a bit of slap and tickle. Even as a gay man I have to admit that when it comes to bumpity-bump, women are very well designed.

Another major bonus of keeping on my apartment was that when Jane's children came to Granny's for a sleepover or a weekend, I could fade back into my own lair. Also when Gregory and his brood arrived from Toronto I could make myself scarce. And when friends came to visit Montreal, provided we considered them housebroken, there was an apartment at their disposal. I suppose running two establishments could be called an extravagance; but as Elinor herself was fond of saying, "It's only money."

My reason for visiting the house this morning was first to collect the mail, and second to pick up Elinor's rolodex. Still firm in my determination to have the party for Elinor, I had to have the list of her friends. I might also invite a few of my own, for comic relief, as well as those we shared in common. Like most men, I choose my friends from among those people I enjoy being around. Men and women who recharge and stimulate me, regardless of age, are those I consider friends. Elinor, on the other hand, maintained friendships with a number of people I would have considered very high maintenance, individuals whose idea of a relationship is centric, with themselves at the centre. So long as their egos are being massaged, their demands met, their whims catered to, the friendship sails through untroubled waters.

One of the downsides to any ongoing close relationship, be it marriage, what used to be called an "affair," or even same-sex arrangements, is that each partner arrives with a great deal of baggage. This freight can take the form of family, friends, business or sports associates (those tiresome men with whom one plays golf or squash but avoids for lunch), hobbies, collections, and furniture. All this accumulation can take a great deal of getting used to.

At the best of times marriage, in the conventional sense, is a difficult undertaking. Elinor and I managed better than most; but, with one or two notable exceptions, I found most of her friends uphill work. Let me hasten to add the friends were less at fault than I. All were willing to accept Elinor's new husband at face value and welcome him into the charmed circle. It was I who resisted being welcomed. The dividing line between warm, solicitous, caring, and just plain nosey is finely drawn. Gatherings of Elinor and her cronies, most of whom were female, turned into good natured grillings. How come I had waited so long before marrying again? Had I broken many hearts? How come we never saw you, a dream escort, at the Museum Ball, St. Andrew's Ball, the Charity Ball? Have you ever been on the board of the S.P.C.A., Welfare Federation, the Montreal Symphony? Didn't we meet at Cynthia's Christmas cocktail party?

For a while, I fielded these questions with tactful evasions. The truth might have set me free, but I did not wish to put Elinor on the spot. The idea of putting on tails to dance with a series of women, most of whom are too busy talking to pay attention to rhythm and steps, is not my idea of a jolly time. To attend committee meetings where members trot out their particular hobby horses is less than stimulating. Hell may well turn out to be a long-winded committee meeting that lasts for eternity. As for cocktail parties, regardless of season, who can be expected to remember people met in tandem with whom one has a three-minute conversation conducted in a quiet scream. As a result, when Elinor met her friends for dinner, I took refuge in my apartment. The solution might not have been to everyone's taste, but it worked for us.

The house had been occupied by Gregory and his wife, who had come to Montreal for the funeral. At my urging they left their children, along with Jane's, at home. A funeral is no place for the young. My statement for the press is that no adult occasion is a place for children, unless heavily sedated. Gregory and Laura protested; shouldn't the grandchildren be present at Granny's funeral? But I was firm. No doubt one day the children will heap blame on their step-grandfather for denying them their grandmother's funeral and the resulting personality dysfunction requiring expensive therapy, but by that time I will be dead and safely out of reach.

There was one other rule to be followed to the letter: The house was to be left exactly as found, meaning nothing was to be taken as memento. Death brings out the latent larceny in families, and I did not want Elinor's jewellery tooling down the 401 in Laura's handbag. Ditto her camera, binoculars, Hermès scarves, Sheffield tray, jade Buddah, or Georg Jensen silver. Elinor had left detailed instructions about who was to get what, and I had every intention of seeing her instructions carried out. Nor did I want to be arbiter in a Tong war when Jane discovered that her sister-in-law had made free with the contents of the sideboard.

For myself I wanted nothing. Elinor had become part of my life, and I did not need alabaster urns or her morocco-bound edition of Jane Austen as a reminder. I kept the wedding ring I gave her, a broad gold band which she had worn. I also wanted a few photographs at which I would never look, a polished stone we found one day at the beach, a handsome brass pot we stumbled across at a flea market, a key chain purchased with pennies she had culled from the loose change we kept on the dresser, and the copper bracelets she sometimes wore to ward off arthritis. These and a few other odds and bits were what I would take, objects of no intrinsic worth but redolent of our life together.

At my suggestion Elinor had left the house to her daughter Jane, meaning that as Westmount residents the children would have access to the library and recreational facilities of which the city was justly proud. Gregory and his wife were to have first pick of the contents, but only after individual bequests to friends. A portion of Elinor's portfolio would also go to Gregory as compensation for his sister's acquiring the house. What remained was to be divided equally, with me as the ultimate arbiter. Elinor had wanted to leave her income in trust to me, the capital going to the children on my death, but I persuaded her otherwise. The extra money would enable Jane and Gregory to offer their children private schools, music and ballet lessons, private tutoring if necessary, and their own computers, thus removing one source of friction. As a single man with no responsibilities I did not need Elinor's money;

I had enough of my own. What I really wanted, very badly, was Elinor herself, but that was no longer an option.

I let myself into the house, fortunately empty but still echoing of Gregory and Laura's having stayed. I was glad. A house left vacant goes stale, and while Elinor lay in the hospital I returned to the relative security of my own apartment. Everything seemed in order. Naturally suspicious, I checked the contents of Elinor's jewel case against a list I had made, only to find everything in place.

Besides the master bedroom there were three other bedrooms on the second floor, one of which Elinor had made into an office. On the walnut kneehole desk sat her rolodex, which I put into the tote bag I had brought. I also opened the bottom drawer to find both camera and binoculars in place. Mail had been stacked neatly on a small table in the entrance hall; I tucked it into the tote to be sorted through at home. Before turning on the alarm and letting myself out, I took a look around. Elinor had taken an ordinary row house: entrance hall, living room, stairwell, dining room, passage leading into the kitchen, and turned it into a personal and welcoming space. Her taste ran to traditional, with slightly worn oriental rugs, upholstered chairs, a couch resting on claw and ball feet, and mahogany occasional tables. Only the coffee table, a frankly Sixties construction of teak with softly rounded edges, did not blend into the room. Elinor had laughingly explained that after all the coats of linseed oil she had applied over the years she couldn't bear to give it up. For just a moment I wondered whether I should lay claim to the table, but reconsidered. I did not need the piece, and I had sure as hell passed the age for wiping linseed oil onto furniture. The table was now Jane's responsibility.

With a feeling bordering on relief, I locked up the house and retraced my steps to the apartment. By now the combination of air, exercise, and food had begun to persuade me I might even live. The hangover had given way to something I imagined to be accidie, a kind of all-encompassing apathy that, so I have read, used to afflict medieval monks living in chilly cloistered cells. Who could blame them?

I nodded to the porter on duty and went to pick up my own mail. On the walk over, I had been mulling over the party. I would hold it at the Lord Elgin Club for two reasons. To begin with, my apartment was too small to accommodate the number of people to be invited. Also I did not want to deal with the aftermath of dead drinks, overflowing ash trays, crumbs in the furniture, and food ground into the rugs. I had decided mid-November would be a good time for the occasion, preferably on a Friday night. That would give those who really tied one on a full weekend to recover. Nor would I be in competition with all the Christmas parties, sing-alongs, *Messiahs*, auctions, bazaars, and the rest of the cant engulfing that most tiresome of seasons.

"Strike while the iron is hot," my father used to say. I once asked him if he had ever been in a smithy. He laughed and replied only when he took his grandfather's horses to be shod, an answer that shut me up. Even without a horseshoe and anvil

I struck, calling the manager of the Lord Elgin to reserve a Friday evening in November. To my agreeable surprise, he told me he had just received a cancellation for Friday, November 19. Would that date be satisfactory? Indeed it would. I sketched in the kind of evening I had in mind: an open bar, perhaps two or three open bars, with club staff passing trays of substantial finger food without letup, enough so that guests would not feel obliged to head out for dinner afterwards. What I had in mind were individual quiches and tourtières, large shrimp dipped in batter, chicken livers wrapped in bacon, cocktail sausages in pastry, and chunks of fried chicken. I also wanted thickly sliced smoked salmon on brown bread and individual servings of steak tartare, if the kitchen could manage it. No salmonella. What I did not want to see were soggy crackers with a rosette of fish paste, anything to do with sardines, a critical mass masquerading as paté surrounded by slices of slightly stale baguette, leaves of endive with a dab of caviar at one end, or cubes of bright orange cheese impaled on toothpicks. I suppose in answer to the health food crowd there would have to be a tray of crudités: carrot sticks, inch long pieces of celery, unpitted olives, clumps of broccoli, and radishes carved into rosettes, all surrounding a bowl of ominous dip.

The manager wanted approximate numbers. I agreed to let him know as soon as possible, but I expected to send around one hundred invitations, possibly more. We had plenty of time to fine-tune the arrangements. What mattered was that I had both a date and a location.

On the walk back to my apartment from Elinor's house I had decided that I would mail invitations with an R.S.V.P. Regrets only. To invite people by telephone, each call entailing a riff on poor dear Elinor, would tie me up for the next three weeks. Already composed in my head, the invitation was to be simplicity itself. "Come and celebrate Elinor. Friday, November 19 at 6:00 p.m. at the Lord Elgin Club. R.S.V.P. Regrets Only." I did not want to call the occasion a "party," a word associated in my mind with birthdays and those hideous gatherings of other children I endured as a child. I wanted to avoid the word "life," with its obvious antonym lurking in the background. I decided only to use her christian name, "Elinor Richardson" being too formal, too redolent of the cemetery. And I would put only the starting time of six p.m. so that guests would not begin to feel uneasy around half past eight. The club staff could deal with the late stragglers.

Still striking before the iron cooled, I telephoned a printer I knew, as I had given him regular business before I retired from my law office. Could he do a small job for me, expense no object? There are times when money not only talks, it declaims. At the right price all things are possible, and I agreed to drop by early tomorrow morning to place the order. More important, I could pick up the appropriate envelopes to begin the task of typing in addresses. Were I to write these addresses in my wayward cursive, the envelopes might end up anywhere from Three Rivers to Kamloops. It was at this point that I might have turned to Elinor to observe that arrangements were progressing nicely. The sobering truth was that Elinor would no longer nod her head approvingly, precisely the reason for the occasion. I derived some chilly comfort from realizing that were she to have been there she would have nodded approvingly. Little did I ever imagine that I would seek consolation in the subjunctive tense.

There remained the thorny problem of the guest list, just who and who not to invite. Between us, Elinor and I knew a lot of people. Our Christmas cards, written by Elinor, went to the post office in a shopping bag. We both had A-list friends, along with B and C. By the time you get to D and below, the ties that bind are pretty loose. Then there is the category of people one actually dislikes; Elinor and I called it our Preparation H list.

It was then that I hit upon the idea of consulting that glum register visitors to the funeral establishment are asked to sign. I suppose people want to be given credit for having shown up, particularly if they have to duck out right after the service for pilates or pedicures. But as you enter the *soi-disant* parlour or chapel, there is the open book, on a lectern, often with a pen attached by a cord or a chain, silent testimony to the eternal truth that in the midst of life we are in theft. I always sign obediently, as though I were registering for a conference or a seminar. Yet that cheerless volume with its black cover and printed lines with a sequence of signatures was to serve as the guest list for my rout. I had been given the book by the funeral director after I had seen the last mourners out. Since they already had my cheque for the service, they were all affability, even offering to drive me home in the company limo.

Seated at my dining table, which could seat six without adding leaves, I spread out my lined pad, my rolodex, Elinor's rolodex, and the funeral register to begin work on my list.

Lionel Adamson: There but for the grace of God goes God. He was a close friend of Elinor's first husband. Formerly a professor of philosophy, Lionel married a rich widow and came to realize a world cruise was more entertaining than lecturing on Plato's *Republic* to restive undergraduates. He has a flinty integrity that is admirable but exhausting; he can find a difficulty for every solution. But he worked tirelessly to de-merge Westmount from the rest of Montreal, and he did come to the funeral. He makes the list in spite of the fact that he will haunt the party wearing the expression of a vegetarian at a barbeque.

Cecily Alford: I knew her years ago, when I had a boyfriend who worked in the theatre. Cecily used to be on the stage, but I always found her to be more of an act than an actress. Onstage she worked with two expressions, happiness and indigestion. Offstage everyone within earshot becomes a member of her captive audience. Now long past the first bloom, she dresses like a female impersonator, too much makeup and false eyelashes that threaten to trip her up. She is good value at a party, however, as she always throws herself into overdrive and creates little eddies of animation. She came to the visitation in a black anorak and wept her mascara into streaks. Of course she will be invited.

Manuel Alvarez: One of my friends. A drop dead gorgeous

Mexican who works as a translator from Spanish, or Spicspeak as he calls it, into French. He is a complete anomaly, a gay man who has absolutely no opinion about curtains. We have never been lovers, but over the years, when we were between entanglements, we would get together for a mercy fuck. It's wonderful to have coloured-lights sex with someone who asks nothing in return, not even a ready ear for his woes. Unfortunately he has developed a tricky heart, which has forced him onto the wagon; but he still loves a party. He came to both the visitation and the funeral. Definitely A-list.

And so it went. Between the visitation and the service there were well over one hundred names in the register. Added to which are the people who telephoned regrets; not a few of their excuses sounded legitimate. Then there will be those who will make donations in Elinor's name to the Cancer Foundation, definitely to be included.

After listing about forty or so names and checking the addresses, not all of which were in the rolodexes, I felt a bit punchy. Last night was still upon me, and I needed a change. Now seemed a good time to check the mail I had carried from the house. I emptied the tote bag onto the table, fetched my letter opener, and began to examine a week's accumulation. There were the predictable bills: telephone, credit card charges, insurance on the house now due, the gardener, who cut the grass and pulled out the most obvious weeds, and the nursing agency for the extra nurses I had engaged for Elinor. Invoices went into a pile to be paid.

An envelope that revealed itself to be a letter was slit open. It was addressed to me at Elinor's address. Odd, as most of my personal mail came to the apartment. The return address, neatly typed on the upper left hand corner, gave a street in Markham. My knowledge of the city is slight, other than it is not far from Toronto. I knew no one who lived there. Opening the envelope, I read.

*Dear Mr. Chadwick,*

*I will be coming to Montreal in early November and would like to meet with you. I have some information that will be of interest to you. Perhaps I could take you to lunch. I will telephone when I arrive.*

*Yours sincerely, Harold Baldwin.*

Under the signature was a telephone number with a 905 area code. Under ordinary circumstances I would probably have telephoned, if only to ascertain whether or not I wanted to meet with said Harold Baldwin. But these were no ordinary circumstances. I knew I would have to cope with a flurry of phone calls from those not coming to the party as well as those offering sympathy in a dark brown voice. These calls nearly always turn into a chat, about poor dear Elinor, about my future plans, about how I was managing, and would I like to come by for a meal. The telephone is an instrument of the Devil, somewhat mitigated by the display window that tells you who is calling. One of the many pleasures of retirement is freedom from the tyranny of the telephone. At the moment I was in no mood to take on new people. The first encounter takes energy, something I found in short supply these days. I decided to leave Mr. Baldwin and his letter in the hands of the gods. The man may or may not call. He may also fall off a bridge, or slip under a bus, or catch something terminal, any of which would spare me the prospect of lunch with a man I felt quite incurious about meeting.

I returned to drawing up my guest list.

Richard Barker: Dick Barker suffers from an allergic reaction to life. Always in some kind of trouble, usually financial, he somehow manages to bob to the surface, in most cases buoyed up by someone else's cheque book. He must owe money to just about everyone on his Christmas card list, a fact that gets him invited to a great many parties as people want to keep tabs on the off-chance he may pay them back. I have kept him at bay by once asking him for a loan. Not that I needed the money, but his predictable turning me down has kept him from subsequently trying to hit on me. In spite of owing money to most of his friends he has never been known to pay for a drink or a meal. Somehow he always has to pee just as the tab arrives. I know he only came to the funeral for the refreshments following the service. Preparation H list.

Felicity Bishop: I will certainly invite Felicity, heart of gold and all. A fading English tea rose, she has never learned, after decades in North America, that incompetence does not equal sincerity and that argument is not the same thing as intelligent concern. How many times have I sat through excruciating meals in her unkempt house while she held forth in her Roedean voice on issues about which her knowledge was slender. Felicity believes not to have an opinion is a sign of weakness. Planned parenthood, American foreign policy, animal rights, waste disposal, subsidized daycare; everything is up for intellectual grabs. I once suggested she save the whales by collecting the entire set. Her reply was to remove my plate without offering me a second helping of bangers and mash. Her heart is in the right place; if only the same could be said of her brain. She came to the service, her hair in a collapsing French roll, her slip visible below her skirt, and too much rouge. She would be wounded beyond measure not to be invited. Do I have any choice.

Charles Bradley: I once had sex with Charles Bradley, after which he told me he really preferred women. *De gustibus non disputandum est.* But I knew I could never get serious about a Presbyterian who has a rosary hanging from his rear view mirror. Not to mention the fact that every time he opened his mouth he changed feet. Charles is very good-looking, in that generic, Sears catalogue way. Totally unthreatening, he draws women almost magnetically. Sadly, he won't even take his own side in an argument, with the result that women move into his life and take over. His apartment has seen more makeovers than the display windows at Ogilvy's. I caught him on the rebound, but was more than happy to throw him back. We have lunch a couple of times a year, once on him, once on me. He

---

33

too knew Elinor's first husband. Although he hovers somewhere between the B and C lists, he did come to the service. To be invited.

When Shakespeare wrote the lines: "O brave new world, / That has such people in't!" he could not have been thinking of my Rolodex.

# 3

*I* took time off from drawing up the guest list in order to take a nap, which turned out to be a three hour stretch of total unconsciousness. I awoke stupefied. Strong tea helped to dispel the fog, and I was just about to continue work on my list when the telephone rang. The display panel showed a telephone number I did not recognize. Warily I reached for the receiver.

"Hello?"

"Good evening, sir. Am I speaking with Geoffry Chadwick?"

"This is he," I replied, the correct use of pronoun giving me a temporary advantage.

"My name is Harold Baldwin. I wrote you a letter."

"Yes, you did. I have it right here." I slid out the sheet and unfolded it. "You said you would be coming to Montreal in mid-November."

"I had a change of plans, and didn't have time to write first. I was hoping we might meet."

The voice on the line offered few clues, other than being male and decidedly Canadian.

"This isn't the best time in the world for me, Mr. Baldwin. May I ask what your call is all about?"

"Well, I was going to tell you in person; it seemed more fitting. But — and this may surprise you — I believe I am your son."

I could scarcely refrain from laughing. "If what you say is true, I am more than surprised; I am astounded."

"Now you can understand why I want for us to meet. You are my father, after all."

I paused for a moment. "Have you proof of such a claim? One half of a battered locket? A tearstained deathbed letter? A well-worn signet ring? A faded photograph? How can I be sure you are not an impostor?"

"You slept with my mother, Jane Blake, one month before she married James Baldwin. I was born seven and one half months after the wedding. As she and James Baldwin had not been together for over a month prior to the wedding, and since she had — dated — no one but you, the presumption is pretty strong that you are my biological father."

The tone was slightly imperious. I suspected Harold Baldwin did not like to be challenged.

Again I suppressed laughter. "I suppose we could have our DNA tested, although I don't know how. Would we have to open a vein, like heros of bygone times, and mingle our blood?

All in the presence of a white-coated lab technician, it goes without saying."

"I don't think we will have to do anything that radical. The blood from a razor cut would suffice. However, according to Mother, there is a strong family resemblance. Of course, she remembers you as a student."

"I see. Tell me, Harold — I presume I may call you that — how old are you?"

"Fifty, on my next birthday."

"May I ask what took you so long to reveal yourself, as it were, to your — your progenitor?"

"I only just found out. Mother has not been well. She suffers from bouts of senile dementia punctuated by moments of extreme lucidity. She blurted out the truth only a short time ago. Look, Mr. Chadwick, I know this is a bit much to absorb over the phone. That is why I would like to have lunch, if you will agree to meet."

"My curiosity is piqued. If indeed you are my — projection into time and space, it would be churlish of me not to meet with you. When are you coming to Montreal?"

"I plan to take an early flight tomorrow morning."

"Than how about lunch tomorrow?"

"That would be fine."

"Come by here about noon. We'll have a drink or a glass of wine. There are a couple of restaurants within walking distance. By 'here' I mean my own apartment. I have two addresses, but I won't go into all that just now. It's a bit complicated, but

I assure you I'm not running a gambling den, a crack house, or a bordello."

Laughter came down the line. "I'm relieved to hear it. We all want our parents to be paragons of virtue. I'll be there at noon."

I gave him the address and paused while he wrote it down. We said goodbye, and I pressed the OFF button on my portable phone.

Well, well, well, Geoffry Chadwick, it has been an action-packed two days. In less than forty-eight hours you have buried a wife and discovered a son. I traded in my tea for a scotch. We all know the past is there, but seldom in the guise of a forty-nine-year-old man who claims you as his father.

The telephone rang again, but I did not answer. I had more than enough news to cope with this evening. If the call were important there would be a voicemail message. And I wanted no more surprises, of any kind, for the moment. Unwilling to face the wasteland of TV, I went back to work on my guest list, working my way methodically through the undertaker's ledger and my Rolodex cards. I came across the names of a few people who had died, and removed their cards from the file. A couple of names were a complete mystery, the person behind the name and address a blank. Former tricks perhaps? I figured they could be safely discarded. Finally, the list neared completion, with only a few names left to check.

Roger Young: Long ago Roger wanted to audition for the role of Queen, but the job was already taken. A shame really, because he has genuine grandeur, in spite of a voice full of ciga-rettes. To begin with, he is tall. I am tall, but Roger is tall enough to be my father. His birthday may be open to negotiation, but he is keenly aware of the scene. When confronted by bores he pops disturbing questions: "Why are the poor more likeable than the rich? Why do we pray? Don't you consider eternal love demonstrates a shocking lack of imagination?" He wouldn't wear a baseball cap if his life depended on it, not even with a little piece of veil. He is the kind of eccentric who would be right at home in the U.K. In Canada, he is tolerated by people he couldn't be bothered to acknowledge in Wal-Mart. Not everyone wants to have pals. Although Roger was a friend of Elinor's, I always enjoyed having him around, as he made me appear kindly by contrast. Anyone who can say to newlyweds, "Avoid your parents' mistakes; use birth control!" has my full admiration. Without question A-list.

It was done. A couple of minutes before ten p.m. and the national news. There is nothing like a few world disasters to clear the mind before bedtime, particularly when read by an anchor whose blond hair shows dark roots under the harsh lights. After all, a day without malice is a day without sunshine.

Jane Blake, a name floating around in the mists of memory. I had no trouble remembering Jane; it is just that I had not thought, really thought, about her in years. And why should I? If I tried to remember all the brief flings from my now longish life, I would suffer from acute memory overload.

Jane formed part of a group I hung out with as a university undergraduate. She hailed from Ottawa, and arrived in Montreal already engaged. More precisely, she had been "pinned," meaning she wore her young man's fraternity pin in lieu of a ring. Her putative fiancé, also from Ottawa, had gone off to Kingston to study. They met periodically on visits home for family holidays and family events. To be at once engaged and separated may be the best formula for this public declaration of intent. The couple is spared the petty annoyances and small erosions of daily contact. Every meeting becomes a kind of holiday, the encounter charged with the sexuality born of prolonged separation. To be young, supposedly in love, and apart for weeks at a time means never having a headache or not being in the mood. And so did Jane manage to sustain her engagement for the four years necessary to earn a B.A., the degree that is more show than substance.

I knew her from around campus; on occasion we found ourselves enrolled in the same courses. Never a genius, Jane worked hard, especially as she did not date, her "pinned" status being common knowledge. By spending evenings in the library, while other girls were learning about life with a capital "L," she managed to pull off regular As with the occasional B+.

Being an out-of-town student, Jane was required to live in Princess Alexandra Hall, the university residence for female students, where they found themselves chaperoned to within a centimeter of their lives. After a year at Princess Alexandra (or PAH as it was commonly known), the girls would have found a Carmelite convent to be lax. Weeknights the residents had to be in the building by ten-thirty p.m. Twice a month they could stay out until one a.m., and once a semester they could come in at two-thirty a.m. The general idea seemed to be that were a young woman to stray down the garden path, she must do so sometime between ten p.m. and the witching hour. No provisions restricting the *cinq-à-sept* were in place, other than those of institutional meal hours. On the plus side, Princess Alexandra boasted the best dining room of any university residence. An invitation to PAH, boys being allowed by invitation only into the dining hall, was seldom refused.

How quaint it seems now, rooted in the tradition that purity was without doubt a woman's most precious asset. "Hello, World, I have an M.B.A. from Harvard and a law degree from Osgoode Hall; I earn $100,000.00 a year; but — above all else — I am a virgin!" That was then. Today a woman's "precious treasure" is her blue chip portfolio, plus her earning capacity and retirement benefits.

I digress. During my college years, Princess Alexandra did not figure largely on my agenda. Like most of the Princess Alexandra residents, I too was experimenting with boys, but I did not have to be "in" by ten-thirty. However, I did date girls on occasion. There are only two sexes, so why limit oneself. It was all so long ago, time measured not only in decades but, more important, in attitudes. When I was at college there was a saying to the effect that the only thing worse than being found in bed with a live man was being caught with a dead woman. Within five decades politicians now flaunt their gaydom as a vote-getting device. Lesbians stump for marriage. Gay men adopt children. It now seems like another century, when the guilty and shameful secret was having a crush on the gym teacher.

Our undergraduate years drew to their inevitable close. The future beckoned, and we raced towards it. I headed into law school; Jane was destined for marriage and children; others went to graduate school, to Europe, to work. A few chose to learn a trade, nursing or carpentry, and knew they would always have a job. So with equal parts gladness and sadness we prepared to say "so long" to our dear old alma mater, "nestled so peaceful and calm 'neath the hill."

A Princess Alexandra Hall tradition was to hold a graduation ball for the departing girls. The affair, a bit daring for the times, was a Sadie Hawkins dance, meaning the girls were at liberty to invite their escorts. Our gang, several of whom lived at PAH, planned to make up a table. Not surprisingly, Jane expected to go with Jim Baldwin, the man whose pin she had worn for four years on her sweater set beside the single strand of graduated pearls she had been given upon graduating from high school.

Some sort of glitch intervened. It all happened so long ago that I no longer remember what, but Jim Baldwin could not make it down to Montreal for the ball. Jane was naturally disappointed, but resigned herself to not going. Without an escort she would feel like a fifth wheel. I speak of earlier times, when unescorted girls were wallflowers who sat in a pastel row looking wanly at the dance floor and hoping desperately to be asked to dance. It was then that one of the girls in our group, the kind of girl who turns out as cheerleader and campaigns for student council, suggested that since I was not going steady at the moment I might escort Jane to the ball.

As a matter of fact, I was going steady at the moment with a teaching assistant, a sensitive young man who seduced me while pointing out my carefree use of the comma in a paper on Milton. However I had no objection to escorting Jane, whom I genuinely liked; and the party of four couples took shape.

The idea of my squiring Jane came as a last-ditch solution, so she had not given any real thought to a ball gown. I came fully prepared, as my mother believed every young man should have tails hanging in his closet, along with a dinner jacket, a navy blue blazer, double-breasted preferably, along with gray and white flannels, depending on the season. Jane, however, did not have a ball gown; furthermore, she did not have a great deal of money. Her solution, North American and pragmatic, was to purchase several yards of ivory satin and a pattern so she could make the gown herself.

The pattern itself was classic and simple, a halter top feeding into a full skirt, to be worn with a belt or sash to conceal the join of bodice to bottom. At the beginning all went well. With the help of other girls on her floor Jane snipped and stitched and sewed, until all that remained to complete was the hem. Her initial plan had been to run the skirt through a sewing machine; but, as she later explained, the heavy fabric bunched and puckered; the end result looked not unlike the hem on *portières*.

—

The girl who lived across the hall from Jane came up with a solution, namely a kind of dressmaker tape one applied to the edge of the fabric with a hot iron. Heat sealed the turned-under fabric in place; moreover, it was fast and easy to apply. In short order, Jane bought the tape, heated up her iron, and applied the adhesive strip around the circumference of the skirt. And not a moment too soon, as the ball was a scant two days away.

By making a few discreet inquiries I learned that Jane's favourite flowers were camellias, especially after seeing a local production of *La Traviata*. The local florist could not rise to camellias, but did supply me with three handsome gardenias, all wired together and topped with a white taffeta bow into which were stuck two lethal, pearl-tipped pins to anchor the construction to the gown.

About the ball itself what can I say. I wore my dinner jacket, or tux, as the other young men did not have tails. We all carried a flask, and sneaked off to the men's toilet to sip. The main lounge had been cleared of furniture and a man hired to play 45 rpm records on a Hi-Fi turntable. I danced with Jane, then dutifully with the other girls in our party. I rather enjoyed dancing were I not required to converse at the same time. I can walk and chew gum, sugar-free naturally; but I cannot keep track of the beat and carry on an animated conversation. Trips to the toilet for sips helped considerably, considering the alternative was a non-alcoholic punch whose main ingredients seemed to be grape juice and ginger ale on top of which slices of orange and lemon drifted aimlessly.

I suppose we were having a good time. Youth is less critical of banal occasions, and we had the boundless energy that dissipates with the passage of time. Friends dropped by our table to visit. We chatted and laughed and took a few turns around the floor. I did not jitterbug, but watched with amusement as a few kinetic couples worked themselves into a lather. We all applauded. It was cheerful and corny and, in retrospect, just a little bit touching. Life had not yet happened to that roomful of young people, and the optimism was so palpable we could have danced on it.

Then a minor disaster struck. From my present perspective it seems frankly comical; but although youth may fake bravado, a quivering insecurity hovers just beneath the veneer. Jane excused herself "to powder her nose," and as she left the ballroom I noticed she was trailing what appeared to be a long strand of fettucini from the hem of her skirt. I hurried after her to point out the problem, and she fled into the washroom to check out the damage.

The explanation turned out to be simple. Satin is a heavy fabric and slippery to boot; consequently, the iron-on tape had proven inadequate to the task of holding up the hem and come unstuck. That meant that Jane suddenly found her skirt, with its collapsing hem, about four inches longer than originally planned. Either she must walk through the rest of the evening holding up the front of her skirt, like the chatelaine in a Fourteenth Century painting, or attempt a quick and radical repair. We looked vainly around for one of the girls from our party to give her a hand, but they were nowhere to be seen. I suspect they had stepped outside the building with their escorts for a smoke, a sip from the flask, and perhaps a little discreet necking. ("Don't crush my flowers! Don't muss my hair!")

We were standing by the fire stairs when Jane asked me to come up to her room and give her a hand. So caught up were we in the drama of the moment that we chose to ignore or overlook the stern Princess Alexandra injunction, chiseled in stone, against having boys in the rooms. Fortunately Jane lived on the first floor, so we sneaked up to her room unobserved. As a senior she roomed alone, so we were not at risk from an importunate roommate.

Jane's solution, crude but effective, was simply to cut four inches off the skirt and hope it would not unravel too obviously before the dance had ended. As luck would have it, she had borrowed pinking shears while making the dress, and had not yet returned them. She slid off the gown and began to cut, while I held the voluminous folds of the skirt in place. In her wired bra and half slip Jane had the lush look of a Renoir nymph, meaning that she would probably put on twenty-five pounds with her first child and spend the rest of her life intending to take them off.

But, young and flushed with the excitement of the moment, she looked extremely pretty. Try as I might I can no longer summon up details. Colour of eyes? Blue perhaps. Maybe hazel. Colour of hair? Not blonde, not black, not red — and worn in a kind of long bob. Yet there we were, alone together in her room, operating on a higher-than-usual frequency because of the occasion, and aware that we were breaking a major PAH rule.

Ah, cannot we,
As well as cocks and lions, jocund be
After such pleasures?

In the detumescent aftermath of what I can remember as a brief, peppy fuck, we came to realize we were in a potentially perilous situation. Were we to be discovered, Jane might be summarily expelled; and I could face sanctions affecting my graduation. After dressing quickly we decided on a battle plan. Jane would give me an all-clear, after reconnoitering the hall; and I would retrace my steps down the fire stairs. If challenged I would say I was looking for the men's washroom. After a bit Jane, in her freshly trimmed skirt, would sweep down the main staircase and join us at our table.

That night He must have taken His eye off the sparrow long enough to see us both safely down to the ground floor, our escapade camouflaged by the crowds and confusion of the occasion. The prolonged absence of one of the other couples at our table drew attention from us, and we played the rest of the evening in low. As that dreary woman says at the end of *To The Lighthouse*, which we were reading in lit class, "I have had my vision." Well, to paraphrase, "We have had our adventure." So we sat, supine and passive, until one o'clock struck and the ball officially ended.

—

I vaguely remember that I was the only young man in our party without a condom or "safe" in his wallet. I had neither expected nor intended to "make out." When I mentioned the lack to Jane, even as I made familiar with her rose coloured nipple, she muttered that she was due any day now. And that was the end of that.

Shortly after the academic year ended and we all graduated, Jane married James Baldwin. She invited me to the wedding, but I decided it would be more tactful to stay away. I sent regrets, along with a Waterford decanter, one of those dumb, useless wedding presents English Canada unloads on newlyweds, along with toast racks, iced tea spoons, silver plated chafing dishes, and finger bowls. At least the decanter could have been turned into a lamp.

After the wedding Jane, now Mrs. James Baldwin, moved to Toronto where her husband had landed a job with a big oil company. Jim was considered to be a young man on the move, meaning he was prepared to stifle any real individuality and become a team player. From what I learned, via the grape-vine, he prospered. Children were born. He moved steadily up in the company hierarchy and coached junior hockey. He voted conservative and went to church on Sundays. After a few years he joined AA and put on weight. Such information as I learned came from mutual friends who kept in touch. I did not. The last bulletin I had was that Jim had died and Jane had chosen to return to Ottawa to be near the children. I thought of writing condolences, but so many years had elapsed since I last saw them I thought better to let it go.

And now the first child of that marriage was turning up on my doorstep claiming me as his biological father. Maybe he was, maybe not. Time, as they say, would tell.

The clock on my night table told me it was after one a.m. Never a good sleeper, I now doze in fits and starts. The bed, the apartment, my life, all are empty since Elinor moved into palliative care. And staying awake all night won't change a thing. As for counting sheep, where does one start? The only sheep I have ever seen were amorphous creatures glimpsed from a car window. Perhaps if I lived in New Zealand. (New Zealand! Where men are men and sheep are nervous.) Do people ever count goats, chickens — after they are hatched — or cows? How about guests at a party?

I must have slept, as dark had given way to dawn. I got up and made coffee. Tempted, as always, to skip breakfast, I thought of Elinor's injunction. She had insisted I eat a breakfast, not large, but nourishing. I scrambled a couple of eggs to eat with toast in solitary silence. It was a heavy, inert silence. Elinor and I did not speak in the morning, only the most basic and necessary monosyllables; yet the silence was alive with possibilities. We subscribed to two newspapers to avoid conflict. Unlike my sister Mildred, Elinor did not feel obliged to comment at length over news items which had caught her attention. She took for granted that I knew how to read. After coffee, two newspapers, a shower, and then some breakfast, we were prepared to slide gently into conversation. More important than a

—

dowry, childbearing hips, or competence in the kitchen, is the ability a woman has for keeping quiet in the morning. Her price is far above rubies.

Shortly after nine I entered the printer's office to order my invitations. I chose a four-by-six ivory card with an embossed border and a simple typeface that in itself made no statement. (How I detest invitations in Gothic script, convinced as I am that I will misread the message and turn up on the wrong day.)

"Is it for a birthday?" asked the printer, a taciturn man with a closed, Presbyterian face.

"No, it's a memorial occasion for my late wife."

"I'm sorry to hear it, Mr. Chadwick. I didn't know Mrs. Chadwick had been ill."

"It was all rather sudden ..." I broke off, unwilling to supply details.

"Tell you what, Mr. Chadwick, I'll charge you only for the cards and envelopes at cost."

Touched by this unexpected gesture, I protested. "That's very kind, but quite unnecessary. I will be quite happy to pay the regular charge."

"No, no, Mr. Chadwick, I insist. You've been a good customer. It's the least I can do."

I thanked him, we exchanged a few inconsequential remarks, and I left with two boxes of envelopes in a shopping bag.

On the way back to my apartment I took a detour to a small grocery store run by Koreans who never seem to take a holiday. While the rest of us are opening gifts, embracing the new year, hunting for eggs, or celebrating the harvest, they are there from dawn to dusk, unfailingly pleasant and helpful. I know they charge more than the large supermarkets; but — keep this under your hat — I don't give a damn. A penny saved usually turns into a colossal waste of time, and I am convinced that penny is far better off making the economy run. For my sins I ran into Harriet Baines, walking testimony to the sad fact that closed minds do not necessarily mean closed mouths. At best a flat-shoe type, she had dashed out in a track suit and rollers. Her father and my father were second cousins, a tenuous connection at best; but she has always presumed to claim kinship.

"Geoffry, it's been ages since I saw you last. My sincerest condolences. I was quite devastated to hear about poor Elinor. I'm sorry to have missed the funeral. My car broke down on the way; I had to be towed, so I missed the service."

"It's the thought that counts," I said lamely, squirming inwardly.

Harriet laughed her social laugh, five "ha's" on a descending scale. "Wouldn't you know I'd run into you looking like this. Just popped out to buy a few supplies: club soda, tonic, crackers. I'm having a few of the girls in for bridge this afternoon, hence the curlers. Do you know," she dropped her voice, "that these people no longer let me bring my dog into the store."

"Isn't there a by-law about dragging your pet dog, or goat, or llama into a food store?"

"I suppose, but still. I am a regular customer. I worry about leaving Hamlet tied up outside."

Through the window I could see the surly brute, part German shepherd, part Boxer, standing aggressively beside the bicycle rack where he had been tied. "I wouldn't worry, Harriet. Not even the Hell's Angels would try to steal him."

Harriet shrugged. "I do regret missing the service. Elinor was such a dear."

"I'm planning a memorial party instead of a service, at the Lord Elgin Club. I'll send you an invitation. Haven't you moved?"

"Yes, I have. Since Ed died I found the house way too big — and depressing. I've moved into a condo, only a block or two from here." She paused to fish around in a shoulder bag trimmed with magenta wool fringe, unfortunate souvenir of a cruise. "Here's my new address. Now you won't forget, will you!"

Her question came out as a command. I nodded an acknowledgement, paid for my purchases, and escaped. What the hell! She did make the effort to attend the service. Also she goes into overdrive at parties and will help carry some of the bigger bores.

# 4

$\mathcal{T}$he hands on the dial of my Rolex made a single line point-ing at twelve when the doorman called to say a Mr. Harold Baldwin was downstairs.

"Please ask him to come up."

"Yes, Mr. Chadwick."

Curiosity mingled with faint apprehension caused me to open the door to my apartment before the bell rang. I heard the eleva-tor door slide open and a man walked down the passageway.

I held out my right hand. "Harold Baldwin, I presume?"

"I am not Dr. Livingstone, so I must be." He shook my hand with a firm grip. "However I am at a loss about how to address you. 'Mr. Chadwick?' 'Father?' Or 'Geoffry?'"

"Geoffry will do nicely, thank you. 'Mr. Chadwick' sounds as though you have come to read the meter, and I admit to not feeling very paternal."

Even as I stood aside to let him enter I had to admit the family resemblance was overwhelming: The same tall, slightly stooped figure; the prominent nose with a high bridge, a legacy from my own father; the same blue eyes, so pale they seemed almost gray. The hair, dark and abundant like his mother's, had been cut en brosse, and the figure was bulkier than mine. Still, there was no doubt that I faced a younger version of myself; or, as Elinor used to say with tongue in cheek, "Just the same, only different."

I indicated the living room. "As they say in British sitcoms, 'Won't you pass through?' Now, would you like a glass of wine, or would you prefer a drink?"

"Wine would be good, colour unimportant."

"That's easy. At least you don't want a piña colada or a tequila sour."

"I'm not even sure what they are, but they sound alarming."

"They are." I pulled the cork from a bottle of Orvieto and carried the wine, along with two glasses, into the living room to find Harold still standing.

"Most people have a favourite chair," he began by way of explanation. "I don't want to get off on the wrong foot by usurping your security space."

I smiled. "Not to worry. When I'm alone I sit in the recliner in the alcove. But seeing as how I have company we'll sit in the lounge, on the three-piece suite." I waved my hand in a broad, sweeping gesture. "Make yourself to home."

"Thank you." I could see him trying not to smile. "Please tell me you don't call this room a lounge."

I laughed out loud, a release of nervous tension. "As a matter of fact I would like to think of it as a parlour, but I don't have a piano. You need a piano in a parlour, preferably draped in a Spanish shawl. And my wife and I never got around to putting our wedding picture into a silver-plated frame to sit on said piano. I can't call it a rec room because I don't have a dart board."

The younger man smiled. "Whatever the name it is a pleasant room. Will your wife be joining us for lunch?"

"Unfortunately no. She died only recently."

"Oh, I'm sorry to hear that. I had no idea. Perhaps you don't feel up to having lunch with a total stranger."

"Not at all. Elinor had been ill for some time. And now she is dead. Nothing changes that. Why would I pass up the chance to have lunch with my son, if indeed you are. Anyway, cheers!" I raised my glass.

As Harold lifted his I could see he had my hands, broad, with long fingers and square nails. His right ankle rested on his left knee, the way I used to sit before arthritis began imposing limits. The apple and the tree and so forth.

"Well — if you're quite sure."

"I am." I set down my glass. "Now, how about filling in some of the background, in broad strokes. I am incurious about your birthday parties and experiences at summer camp. You can skip over your first kiss, first drink, first cigarette, first lay. In other words, let's begin from the present and work backwards."

———

Harold laughed quietly. "Before I begin, do you mind if I smoke?"

"No, the crystal whatnot on the table is an ashtray."

"You're sure you don't mind?"

"Only cigars. The smell lasts for days. Elinor was not a smoker, and neither am I. But many of our friends still smoke. The over-fifties find it hard to give up."

Harold took out a half empty pack of cigarettes and a lighter. The first drag went down to his navel. "A cigarette helps with stress. And meeting your father for the first time rates fairly high on the anxiety index." He inhaled a second time. "Now, in broad outline, I am a teacher by profession, high school English, although currently between jobs, read unemployed. I am divorced. If you are prepared to accept me as your son then I come with two grandchildren, a boy and a girl, you don't really want to know. Actually they're not bad kids, just monumentally uninteresting. Their principal concerns are clothes, the internet, scraping through school with a minimum of effort, and low-carb diets. They also move through life in a hormonal haze, but I have them brainwashed into abject terror of unwanted pregnancies and STDs. They will be scarred for life, but they may make it through to adulthood without major mishaps. They live with their mother, a well-meaning but limited woman, who does what she can, which isn't much."

"Let's leave the grandchildren for the next chapter. I haven't yet adjusted to the idea of having a son. One generation at a time. How come you're not working?"

We had both drunk our first glass of wine quite rapidly, as neither of us felt at ease. But so far so good. Any parent who doesn't think the sun shines out of his child's ass can't be all bad.

Harold gave a dismissive shrug. "The simple answer is that I quit. The more detailed explanation is that I am having a mid-life crisis, details to follow; and I took a year's leave of absence. That sounds less perfunctory than saying 'I quit,' but I have no intention of going back. My putative father, James Baldwin, devoted his life to the business of business. When he died he left his children an annuity; and when Mother dies, his estate, left to her in trust, will come to us. As a result, I am in the enviable position of not having to work."

I refilled our glasses. "How will you pass your time? Writing a memoir? Growing orchids? Making your own wine? Or simply smoking and drinking the days away in front of the telly?"

"None of the above. After a few months of wallowing in the mid-life crisis, which I suppose is another way of taking a holiday, I fully intend to find something to do, something constructive I mean. The question is what."

I repressed a laugh. "You're a bit old for the Peace Corps. And the World Food Program ships you off to places you may want to visit but not to live. You're not yet old enough for Meals-on-Wheels. How about teaching English as a second language?"

"What do you think I've been doing for the last fifteen years to supposedly English-speaking students in Toronto? I would have had an easier time with Mandarin, or Old Norse, or Huron."

We both permitted ourselves a laugh, this time with a little mirth to leaven the tension.

Harold uncrossed his legs and leaned forward. "I seem to be making a 'new beginning,' as the ads say; and since Mother blurted out the truth about my parentage, I decided to look you up. New beginning, new parent, new life. *Quo vadis?*"

"How about out to lunch? If I drink more wine I would prefer it to be with food."

"Sounds good," said Harold, and stood, but not before sliding his second, still unlit, cigarette back into the package. "I wasn't sure about the dress code, so I figured a tie would see me through most situations. I was torn between stripes and tiny, repeated objects. I chose stripes."

"Good choice. A striped tie is the male equivalent of graduated pearls. Suitable for any occasion, including washing the car. I am old enough to be of the shirt and tie generation, a 'suit' in today's parlance. I wore a tie to private school; I wore one at university; and I always wore a tie at the office. Now that I am retired I only wear one on special occasions, such as my first lunch with Number One Son."

We both managed a laugh, helped along by the wine. I guess we were both flying blind. If there is a chapter in the etiquette books that covers meeting a middle aged son for the first time, I am unaware of it. Where are you Beatrice Fairfax, Emily Post, Ann Landers when we need you most?

I pressed the button for the elderly elevator, and soon we were clanking our way down to the street and into our future.

Had I read the tea leaves, perused the Tarot cards, gazed into the crystal ball, or examined a sheep's entrails, I don't believe I would have seen a bicycle courier speeding through a red light. Filled with rage as he shot past, I cursed him soundly and wished him harm. God must have been listening, as the rider appeared to lose control of his bicycle and sideswipe a moving taxi. Describing a graceful arc through the hazy autumn air, he came to rest on the sidewalk, stunned and supine. Swept with a rush of vindictive adrenalin, I took a moment to realize that Harold too was lying, supine and stunned, on the road.

Shock and pain rendered him almost inarticulate, but he managed to blurt out, "I think my leg is broken," before lapsing into the semi-consciousness of shock. Subsequent events remain somewhat out-of-focus in memory, like a film that has been exposed twice. There were police, an ambulance, and the inevitable crowd of curious gawkers. I answered the questions as best I could: waiting for the light to change, beginning to cross on the green, out of nowhere the bicycle ignoring the red. Where were they taking the two casualties?

It has been observed that the leopard cannot change his spots. Nor can the jaguar for that matter, but to the leopard goes the cliché. Even distressed by the accident and not a little buzzy from two glasses of wine, I could not help noticing that the interrogating officer was drop-dead good looking. (Black hair and blue eyes. Be still, O Heart!) But all I did was notice. After the Urgences Santé paramedics had loaded the bodies on stretchers into the ambulance and driven off, to the Montreal

General Hospital I was assured, I asked the taxi driver who had bounced the bicycle courier off his mudguard if he wanted a fare. Business is business and, ignoring the dents and scratches, he drove me to the hospital, arriving only seconds after the ambulance.

There is about hospital waiting rooms a quality of boredom so pervasive and all-encompassing that anxiety is dulled. I sat motionless, stupefied by Orvieto and shock, and desperate for something to read. Tattered, antique copies of *Time* and *Chatelaine* did not hold my interest. Stale news and a fail-safe marinade for salmon failed to captivate. I felt vaguely hungry without any desire to eat, vaguely anxious without any real wish for answers, and vaguely curious as to whether the courier's mishap had anything to do with my muttered imprecation. My son, whom I now freely acknowledged, was having his leg encased in plaster because some yahoo on a bicycle had chosen to ignore traffic lights. I did not wish the lout dead, only badly bruised and shaken up, enough to make him abandon riding as courier for a nice, safe job stocking shelves at Wal-Mart.

The nagging realization, slow at first to take shape but gaining in size and momentum, that I was going to have a patient on my hands, did not add to my sense of well-being. On the way down in the elevator, Harold told me he was staying in a small hotel not far from my apartment. Unless the leg were damaged enough for him to require hospitalization, he would need a place to stay where he could be cared for. I knew there were rehab hospitals, places where post-operative patients went after being outfitted with new hips and knees. Perhaps Harold would be shipped off to one of these until he could manage on his own. Still, I would have to visit: magazines and books, fruit and candy in a bag, face and voice full of caring concern, and bearing tidings of the outside world.

The problem with this scenario, a major miscalculation by central casting, was that I am not by nature a caregiver. Whatever my virtues, they do not include nurturing the sick and wounded. Visiting hospital rooms clocks in just above a root canal job as an activity I wish to avoid. To be sure, I did care for Elinor, and willingly. But she was my wife, the last and best love of my life, and I gladly did whatever I could to ease her final time. Then she went into palliative care, and I felt deprived, more than deprived, desolated. But, son or not, Harold Baldwin remained a stranger. More than willing to learn to know him over a length of time, I found myself deeply unwilling to be his nurse, cook, and caregiver. Yet the alternative, to shut my door and close him out of my life, struck me as unfeeling, even according to my curmudgeonly code.

As always, there is a bottom line: in effect, what would Elinor have done under the circumstances. She would have welcomed him in; furthermore, she would have bounced me off the walls for hesitating. Did I really have a choice?

All of which helps to explain how I came to be standing over the stove cooking scrambled eggs for breakfast, my most unfavourite meal of the day. The newly rediscovered son, his ankle encased in plaster, lay in my bed in my bedroom. (The trick with scrambled eggs is to add a little water while beating and to cook slowly over low heat. I also added grated parmesan.) The master bedroom had been reluctantly relinquished to the patient as the en suite bathroom was only a few steps from the bed. As well, the eighteen inch commode (a.k.a. toilet) came equipped with arms, installed a couple of years ago when an arthritic knee was giving me trouble. The higher seat, plus the arms, made it possible for Harold to negotiate without my help, a definite bonus, as I did not relish the prospect of pulling him off the loo. The downside was that when I used the second or "house" bathroom, with its fourteen inch toilet, I felt as though I were sitting on a chamber pot. I also had to grab onto the handbasin to pull myself upright, and all this after a long trek down the hall.

The doctor on duty in the emergency unit did a good job of putting the arm on me. Harold could, if absolutely necessary, go to a rehab hospital; but that would mean he occupied a bed which a more seriously injured patient could readily use. Of course, if I really couldn't manage ... But, remember, you can call your local CLSC to send a nurse who will check the cast and help him to wash, dress, and face the day.

My heart of stone turned to pumice, and my newly discovered son came to reside in my apartment until such time as mobility permitted his return to Toronto. No sooner had we accomplished the manoeuver of getting him back to the apartment than I called the CLSC for a nurse to come by the following morning. She arrived promptly at eight, and I did my best to be civil to this unwelcome presence so early in the morning. I had not passed a particularly restful night. Accustomed as I was to sleeping in a queen-sized bed, I had to relearn how to cope in a single. I had awakened around three a.m., groggy, disoriented, and halfway onto the floor. Then a trek down the hall to pee, after which, in a moment of forgetfulness, I flushed. In the dead calm of early morning the appliance emitted a gurgling roar that must have been audible right out to the street. By now awake, I went to check on the patient, only to find him sprawled comfortably across the expanse of my own bed and sleeping the sleep of the unjust. It was all I could do not to wake him, out of sheer spite.

Yet another annoyance was the pervasive smell of cigarette smoke in my bedroom. When I had allowed Harold to smoke, I was anticipating one, perhaps two pre-lunch cigarettes. Obviously I had not realized I would be playing host to a heavy smoker, one who would saturate the apartment with the rancid odour of stale cigarettes. At this point it would be difficult, if not downright inhumane, to impose a No Smoking rule on a committed smoker. I did, however, impose one condition: no smoking in bed. If he wanted to smoke, he must use the bathroom. Not only did I not want my bedding to absorb the odour, I did not want to come riding to the rescue, like young Lochinvar, with a fire extinguisher at one a.m. My injunction came out as an edict, not a request; and Harold agreed to comply.

When the doorbell rang on the stroke of eight, I bared

my teeth in what might have passed for a smile and admitted a woman with very short hair and very long teeth who wore, under her brisk manner of professional good cheer, an air of aggrievement, as though life had dealt her two pairs when the rest of the world held three of a kind. Even as we discussed the business of the patient I suspected that given half a chance she would be more than happy to unburden herself of her predictable problems: the husband who ran off, the children who dropped out of high school, the dotty mother who refuses to take her medication, and the sister who married well and offers financial assistance, but never enough. But to be fair, Janice McSween, the name pinned to her blue uniform, saw Harold expediently through his morning ablutions (shit, shower, shave, as we called them in college), and made certain that nothing untoward was happening under the cast.

As she was preparing to leave, I was tempted to ask whether she was related to Nurse Janice of *The Muppet Show*, the one who assisted Dr. Bob in the Veterinarians' Hospital skits; but I reconsidered. The woman looked not unlike a Muppet herself; she might well take my question amiss, and perhaps maintaining a civil distance was best.

By now the eggs had cooked and bran muffins warmed in the microwave. (Bran muffins to keep "down there" functioning smoothly.) I spooned eggs onto plates, sprinkled a little paprika over top for mise en scène, and carried the food into the dining room where Harold, with the aid of crutches, had installed himself.

"Hey, there, you with the stars in your eyes," I said, setting down the plates.

"Love never made a fool of you. You used to be too wise," he replied with a laugh.

"Very good," I said approvingly. "I have to admit my knowledge of musical comedy is spotty, but Elinor had a number of show records." I laughed out loud. "Part of her dowry, I suppose, and more interesting than goats or gold bangles."

Harold set down his fork. "I hope you realize, Geoffry, how much I regret putting you out like this. I can't thank you enough for taking me in, like a foundling. And I hope one day I can return the favour."

"I appreciate the thought, Harold; but I hope it won't involve my being encased in plaster. Now, the question before the Board is how do we keep the patient happy and occupied. While we bond over your broken ankle, would you like to listen to canned music, read, watch TV? I'm not sure whether we are too late for *Sesame Street*. As an English teacher you may want to keep abreast of the alphabet."

As he swallowed, Harold held up his hands, palms outwards. "Please! You do not have to entertain me. I am quite able to divert myself. I see you have bookshelves, with real books in them. There is a television set in the bedroom, and a radio. My cup runneth over. And believe me, the minute I can manage by myself I'll be out of here."

"Do you have someone to do the heavy lifting when you return to Toronto?"

"Yes and no. I don't live with anyone, at the moment anyway; but I have friends who will bring in groceries and run the occasional errand."

"In that case you'd better not be in too much of a hurry to dash off. The problem is that you are not sick, only incapacitated. This can lead to affirmative bursts of self-sufficiency, which in turn can lead to accidents. Sometimes it is difficult to distinguish independence from bad judgement. Speaking as your father, I don't think you should think of leaving until you are a lot more mobile than at present."

Harold sat bolt upright and saluted as he butted his post-breakfast cigarette. "Yes, Sir! And thanks for breakfast. Now I think I'll lie down for a bit and put my leg up. I feel as though I'm carrying the — the Rosetta Stone on the end of my leg."

"I thought Rosetta Stone was a gospel singer."

"No, that's Hope Diamond."

"On that scintillating note I will do my chores."

Harold pushed himself upright and limped down the passageway. He appeared to be managing well on crutches, and my guess was that he wouldn't be hanging around too much longer.

I have one of those refrigerators that expels ice cubes from what looks like a mechanical anus. I filled a tumbler with ice, added water, and carried it into the bedroom of the patient.

"Thank you, Nurse Geoffry."

"Do mention it. Would you prefer to read? Or shall I do my big sick-room number and draw you out?"

"I'd much prefer to talk, if you have nothing more urgent to do."

"What could be more urgent than making up for forty-nine years of benign neglect? Tell me about your children, in broad strokes. There are limits to my curiosity."

Harold made himself more comfortable, placing a pillow under his knee and banging the pillows behind his head, something I should have volunteered to do; but I am not by nature a pillow-banger.

"Lisa, the eldest, is sixteen. Pretty in a bland, blonde way. Beautiful eyes. By the time she is twenty-five she will have a weight problem. Bright. Does well in school with a minimum of work. She has a good lyric soprano voice and wants to study singing. I got her started on piano so she could at least learn how to count. For a successful career in singing you have to have fire in the belly. I doubt she has the drive, but time will tell. All her mother and I can do is provide the right opportunities. I can't live her life for her, nor do I want to. My long-range forecast is probably marriage, a family, with a job in a choir or a church.

"Jason, the airhead apparent, is three years younger. I think he may be bright; I certainly hope so, but most of the time it's difficult to tell. Between tennis in the summer, squash in the winter, and the internet all year round, we seldom speak, except in monosyllables. I suppose he'll land on his feet. To be good looking and computer savvy is not a bad combination. Are the brush strokes broad enough?"

I smiled. "Quite. You might even volunteer some carefully selected details, as in a high school essay, which will expand these two-dimensional figures into three."

Harold took a sip of ice water. "How to begin?" He began to laugh. "I guess you know more about my beginnings than I ever will."

"Don't sass your Pop. How about beginning 'in medias res,' like those long epic poems I read at university. You too, I should imagine."

"You mean how Grendel sacked Troy before leading the rebel angels against God? I hardly think of my life as epic, but I will skip over the bland childhood. Sadly, I wasn't born in a trunk in the Princess Theatre, so I'll jump to graduation."

The following narrative turned out to be at once quite ordinary in its substance but unusual in its mode of telling. A young man growing up in the city of Markham, Regional Municipality of York, goes to Kingston to university leaving behind a girl studying to be a nurse. After earning an M.A. in English literature, he makes the decision to teach at the high school level rather than pushing ahead for a Ph.D. and a university career. Filled with the boundless optimism of youth, he believes the high school years to be critical in capturing the interest of the future scholar. After growing up and going to university in small cities, he finds himself in Toronto and somewhat at a loss. In the meantime his lady friend has landed a job in a large Toronto hospital. Both finding themselves a bit daunted by the size and impersonality of a large city, they fall back on one another for mutual support. They also fall into bed. It is not the first time in history that the combination of sex and compatibility escalates into what passes for love. With two incomes and no financial responsibilities they are free to choose a future, and marriage happens.

For a while the story continued to unwind in predictable fashion: work, house in the suburbs, mortgage payments, weekends in Markham to visit the family, a baby, general rejoicing, promotion at work with corresponding salary increase, another baby, followed by a long stretch of predictable parenthood.

All of this agreeably banal narrative held the interest of novelty for me. To begin with, the narrator was my newly minted son; secondly, he had lived a life of which I was largely ignorant. After my first wife was killed I sidled out of the closet and spent the rest of my youth and middle years as an openly gay man. Why I married Elinor remains, even to me and some of my closest friends, a quixotic decision; but they would all agree with me that this decision turned out to be the best one I ever made.

Another reason for this tale of young love and marriage in the suburbs to hold my interest sprang in no little wise from the wry, more than wry, acidulous mode of narration. As an English teacher Harold had a way with a word, but his own take on his life managed to reduce the experience to a sitcom. Whatever sense of irony I might have directed at the story found itself undercut by the greater irony of the narrator. Perhaps irony is not the appropriate word. What I heard was a kind of underlying bitterness bordering on misogyny, but delivered with a zing that amused even as it startled.

About his ex-wife he was particularly scathing. As I listened I ticked off the put-downs. She was described as having an hourglass figure, but time is running out. She brings joy whenever she goes. She is as dim as a foreign film; her taste in decoration runs to chintz and tchotchkes. Unfortunately there is no lifeguard in the gene pool because her only culture is bacterial. She loves Nature, in spite of what it did to her, and marriage to her was like the best of all Tupperware parties.

"I did not expect marriage to be a lifetime of unalloyed delight," he added by way of conclusion, "and I am the first to realize that when everything is coming your way you are in the wrong lane; but the reality of daily cohabitation and parenthood blew me off. Wives and children are here today, here tomorrow. And when we decided to divorce I realized that there were three children involved: Lisa, Jason, and my wife."

"Does your wife, my daughter-in-law, have a name? Up to this point she hasn't been given a credit, not even in the list of supporting players."

"Barbara."

"I'm glad to hear it. Up to now she has been a kind of allegorical figure: The Wife, nameless, but with a shopping list of irritating attributes. Let me interrupt this narrative to ask you a question. If she is as borderline awful as you suggest, how come you married her in the first place? I do not think you a fool, so how did you lose your footing so badly you married a woman you appear not to like but to positively dislike?"

Harold made a gesture, something between a shrug and a shiver. He had not been expecting my question, so I could see it had thrown him off-balance.

"I don't have a quick answer to that one."

"Then I do. I've been listening to you, Harold, listening pretty carefully. The reason you claim not to like your wife, or ex-wife, is that you don't much like Harold Baldwin. It's hardly original of me to point out that it is difficult to like other people if you don't like yourself."

Harold shifted position, placing his hands, palms down, on the covers. "You are right. But do you know me well enough to judge how I feel about myself? Also, you don't know my ex-wife, any more than I knew yours. Maybe I don't like myself, but that does not necessarily mean that all my ducks are swans."

"True enough. After all, we have only just met." I laughed in spite of myself. "Believe it or not, I am not given to making fortune cookie or bumper sticker pronouncements. But we have a lot of catching up to do in a very short time. And I can't help feeling your clever put-downs act as a kind of barrier. Look, Harold. I am seventy. My wife and best friend just died. A son, whom I believe you to be, has just sprung, fully grown, into my life; Pallas Athene from the brain of Zeus; and I would like to know where you are coming from. If you would prefer me to skate over the surface you will find me perfectly accommodating. I can discuss the weather, medicare, old movies with the best of them. Furthermore, I will keep my distance. I had hoped for more, but what the hell! Why should you tell me anything."

"What precisely would you like to know?"

I paused just a moment and looked directly into his eyes. "Are you gay?"

He returned my gaze without flinching. "Yes."

I relaxed into my chair and smiled. "Good. Now we can begin to get to know one another."

"Agreed. But first I'm going into the bathroom for a cigarette."

The telephone rang. Although I keep an extension on the night table, I could see the call was long distance; and when the name Lawrence Townsend flashed onto the display screen I decided to answer on the extension in my office.

"Larry?"

"I know you are shrouded in widower's weeds; but remember, Honey, I knew you when."

"Your compassion overwhelms me, as always. What's up?"

"My antennae told me that you were pining for the sound of my voice. And possibly, just possibly, my living, breathing presence. I'm thinking of coming to Montreal. The only way to live in Toronto is to get the hell out once in a while."

"Larry, I can't stop you from coming to visit. But if you are planning an all-stops-out tear then count me out. I am feeling a little fragile these days, which, I suppose, is another way of saying I can cope with you sober but not drunk."

"Why, Geoffry Chadwick, what a thing to say. When have you ever seen me anything more than borderline tipsy? Besides, I'll be on my best behaviour as I will be travelling with someone."

"Is this someone a lower case or an upper case someone?"

"I don't know yet. That's one of the reasons I want to visit Montreal. There's nothing like that romantic little getaway weekend to show up the cracks in a budding relationship."

"True enough. I hope it works out for you. We're neither of us getting any younger. What's he like?"

"Younger — but these days eighty per cent of the North American population is. Tall, and in the dark, good looking. He's square, a veritable cube. He's also hung. His dick has a dick."

"Well, to quote the immortal Shakespeare: 'Some have greatness thrust into them.' Does he know how to read and write? Not all of your former beaux could boast these skills."

"O, ye of little faith. He is a professor, of something arcane and dreary: Anglo-Saxon, Old Norse, Middle English. He can recite reams of *Sir Gawain and the Green Knight*, *Beowulf*, and don't even get him started on *The Canterbury Tales*. And — can you believe — he likes me because I'm not academic. You know me, moving my lips to read the phone book."

"A slight exaggeration, but I take your point. I'll also bet he doesn't mind the fact that you can accelerate from zero to sixty-nine in fifteen seconds."

"Stay as sweet as you are. I'll let you know when he can get away."

"Call again, when you have less time."

—

"Fuck you too, Chadwick. But, to be serious for only a moment, I decided not to come to Montreal for Elinor's funeral. I figured you would have enough on your plate, and with family commitments you would be all taken up. I didn't want to make the trip knowing I would hardly see you."

"You made the right decision. Even if we did have lunch, or a drink, you would have found me poor company. And we have known each other too long for pro forma gestures. Keep in touch."

I replaced the receiver and sat for a moment. Was I up to coping with Larry, Lawrence Townsend II? I have known him since grade school, a duration of time which, I suppose, qualifies him as a friend. In truth, Larry is more of a lifelong affliction, like the heartbreak of psoriasis or the shame of scaly dandruff. How many drunks, nights on the town, trips to the steam baths, and bouts of unseemly behaviour have we shared. Eventually I graduated into a series of stable relationships, while Larry continued to play the field, or the sidewalk. For Larry, a weekend with the same man was a love affair; his idea of fidelity was not being in bed with two people at the same time. Then the scene changed. With more than a little prodding from me he came to realize the only person he was hoodwinking was himself. Between lethal diseases, drugged crazies, and his advancing years, he began to understand that beaded-bagging it into the seedier parts of town was no longer a gas but a risk.

But the ties between us remained strong. Even as youngsters we travelled along parallel tracks. Our fathers and mothers played bridge together; we attended the same private schools; we both went to McGill. In spite of similarities in our backgrounds, there were also major differences. Many of us tiptoed down the garden path; Larry sprinted. I firmly believe he came out of the closet before the onset of puberty. Kindly, older men were forever offering him lifts along the scenic route. He always seemed to have more pocket money than his affluent classmates, but manna from heaven comes in many guises. And who would have thought to question anyone who was always ready to stand treat for a chocolate soda and a caramel sundae. Those were the days when overdosing on sugar brought us closer to God. How things have changed. (When God does acid or drugs does he see people?) I digress.

I returned to the bedroom. "A call from an old friend. Nothing you couldn't have overheard, but I find it tedious to listen to one half of a conversation. Whoever invented the cell phone will have a lot to answer for on Judgement Day."

Harold smiled. "Do you own a cell phone?"

"No, I'm not important enough. I can be reached by regular telephone, regular mail, or messenger. I don't want people phoning me to say they will be twenty minutes late. I want them to be on time."

"Do you have a computer?"

"Yes, but I don't use it much."

"Not even for e-mail?"

"Least of all for e-mail. When I had an office I had a secretary to do my typing. Why play the tape backwards? I find something just a little bit obscene about being available at all times, like a hooker. It is a prostitution of the spirit. And should I lose out on the deal of the century, or the biggest lottery prize in history, or the weekend for one at the Paradise Motel with seventy-two quasi-virgins, then the loss is mine. End of diatribe."

Harold laughed. "It is refreshing to meet someone like you. Most people I know are afraid to take a shower lest someone call while they are too wet to answer. And you're right about importance. Who but heads of state and doctors should be always on call. For the rest of us it is an exercise in vanity."

Harold adjusted the pillow under his leg. "Geoffry, can I presume you are not going to throw me into the street?"

"Whatever for?"

"For being gay."

"Harold, I am not given to quoting scripture, but isn't there a saying to the effect that he who is without sin can cast the first stone? I avoid intimate confessions, least of all with people I scarcely know. But after seventy years of living my life I am not about to cast any stones."

"That's a relief. Attitudes vary from generation to generation, and," Harold sat up abruptly, "I suppose that being my father does move you up one generation from mine. It's odd, but I don't feel as though you are a whole generation removed from me."

"I owe it all to steroids, botox, and polyfilla. Seriously though, I have always believed one reaches a cosmopolitan age, say around forty to forty-five, when age as such ceases to matter.

At that point you should be able to talk to twenty or seventy without feeling put upon."

Harold swung his legs over the side of the bed. "I think I'd like to get up. This is not an easy discussion for me, and I feel at a disadvantage lying here, tucked up like an invalid."

Harold had long, well shaped legs, like mine I was pleased to see. A former lover once told me that my legs would look good in black net stockings, but cross-dressing has never held any appeal for me. Besides, it strikes me as an awful lot of hard work. For a man to pass successfully as a woman requires extensive engineering: struts and supports, things cantilevered, learning to balance on heels. Makeup imposes its own limitations and restrictions, while something as simple as taking a pee becomes a major manoeuver.

We sat at the dining table, whose solid surface helped Harold to sit and stand unaided. Having brought the ashtray and cigarettes, he smoked.

"As long as you are not in the business of passing judgement," he began, "I'd like to tell you about my most recent aberration, or lapse of taste, or departure from judgement."

"In other words, a love affair that went sour."

Harold laughed, a short, hard laugh without mirth. "Once again you have the jump on me. You must think me a bit slow and retarded."

"Not in the least. You don't feel you know me well enough to begin a story without a preamble, a kind of preparation. It is a form of courtesy, and I can live with that. It's just that I can usually read the signs, and so could you were the roles reversed. But go on with your story. I promise not to jump the gun."

"After Barbara and I decided to separate, I met someone. Believe it or not, I didn't run around while I was married, less from virtue, I hasten to add, than from the problem of logistics. When you are teaching a full high school load, coping with two young children, and dealing with the obstacles thrown daily across the path, when do you find time for intimate meetings, trysts, tête-à-têtes, and the rest of the baggage that goes with an affair. Doesn't that word date me. I've never been interested in furtive sex: saunas, back rooms, blowjobs in the bushes, not to mention the risks involved these days in that sort of behaviour. As a result, it was only after I moved out of the family nest that I had time to begin what I believe is called 'dating' again."

"So far what you say makes perfect sense to me. Then what?"

"Then I met someone. I still don't have enough perspective to know whether I was genuinely in love with the man, or whether I was so besotted with the idea of being in love that I had a kind of one-size-fits-all approach to anyone who knew how to use a knife and fork and had a vocabulary of over eight hundred words."

"You are not the first to have faced this dilemma. 'Is it the real turtle soup, or merely the mock?' For a while, at least, things must have seemed promising."

"They did. We both made concessions. He understood I had to spend time with my children." Harold suppressed a laugh. "I learned to overlook his wearing wool socks with Birkenstocks."

"Hardly an indictable offense."

"True enough. But the Devil, as they say, is in the details. After two decades of marriage I was up to my eyeballs once again in domesticity. Not that I wanted to run around, go to bars, whoop it up; but I relished the idea of being free to see movies, attend concerts, go to the opera without having to hire a sitter and plan the evening like a military campaign. Grant — he has a name — Grant liked staying home, cooking meals, renting movies, watching TV. Nesting."

I smiled. "Did any of these home-cooked meals involve noodles, a tin of cream of mushroom soup, and perhaps a tin or two of flaked tuna?"

Harold laughed out loud. "Geoffry Chadwick, you are a profoundly wicked man!"

"I'm glad to hear tuna fish casserole is still on the menu. In my youth it was known as fruit pie, as it was what you were usually served when 'poor but proud' gay couples asked you to dinner. And you bring the plonk. But, we digress. On with your tale."

"As I said, the Devil is in the details, of which I will spare you a lengthy catalogue. Think, or try not to think, of dust ruffles, pillow shams, drop cloths on furniture, doilies under whatnots, calendars with kittens, and souvenir beer stemins. Ignore the braided rugs, sunflower place mats, gingham napkins, and the wicker basket of beach stones — from the Provincetown vacation — on the toilet tank. It was like living in the L.L. Bean catalogue. I soldiered on, wearing blinkers; but one day the crunch came. He wanted to get married."

"Excuse me," I interrupted, trying not to smile, "you mean as in same-sex marriage?"

"Precisely. Having just emerged from one marriage — a sterling silver, Royal Doulton, monogrammed napkin marriage, I was faced with the prospect of moving into a sitcom. Straight eye for the queer guy."

"His and his towels?" I fought down laughter.

"A bridal registry at Costco."

"Enrolling the Asiatic baby you planned to adopt at Upper Canada College?"

"A down payment on a Winnebago."

"Thanksgiving with the in-laws. You will bring the dessert."

Harold clapped his hands together. "And — best of all — now that I have tracked down my real father, you could have given me away."

"Gift wrapping not included."

Suddenly we were off, overwhelmed by laughter that welled up uncontrollably. The raucous mirth had little to do with the minor amusements of decorating disasters. This laughter sprang from something much deeper: denial of illness, grief, emotional disappointment, awareness of mortality, and the sheer shittiness of being alive. I had not laughed this way in months, certainly not since Elinor fell sick. And I suspected, Harold had gone through his share of disappointments and dismay, not to mention a broken ankle. We laughed in defiance, our semi-hysterical

jollity a finger to the universe. And during that temporary sus-
pension of what passes for social decorum, something happened
between Harold and me. None the less tangible for being
unspoken, we came together in a way that might otherwise have
taken weeks, even months, of conventional exchanges. Aside
from the shared complicity of abandoned laughter, I felt something akin to gratitude for this opportunity to push unhappiness
aside, if only for a few moments.

Whether or not he was really my son no longer seemed
important. Harold had entered my life.

## 5

*T*spent a good part of the morning addressing envelopes until it was time to confront the problem of lunch, a tedious meal unless I eat out. Living alone as I do I tend to snack: cheddar cheese and a bagel, a tin of sardines, a couple of fried eggs; but now that I was catering for a patient I felt obliged to provide something that resembled a meal. To be fair, which on most occasions I prefer not to be, Harold was not a picky eater, chowing down happily on whatever I dished up. The obdurate fact remained that dinner is far easier to encompass than lunch. A couple of chops slung into the oven along with a pair of potatoes; a precooked ham with something starchy on the side and a salad bought already shredded; a steak charred on the grill; a slab of haddock saved from scorching by the lazy cook's faithful standby, a tin of mushroom soup; or, when all else failed, a quick call to Chicken Charlie's.

Lunch, however, remained a real pain in the wazoo. Most lunch dishes are fiddly; they demand attention. The soufflé must be watched; the poached eggs, even with store-bought Hollandaise, minded; the tuna melt attended to. Telephoning out for lunch betrays a want of moral fibre, a suggestion that you are throwing in the towel before the fight has started, or climbing into the lifeboat before the ship has sailed. Fortunately, I had bought a quiche yesterday, untroubled by the dictum that real men never eat cheese pie. As we both intended to take a nap, I opened a bottle of cheap and cheerful red wine, than asked Harold if he was ready to eat.

"For someone who claims not to like cooking you are pretty nimble in the kitchen," observed Harold as he lowered himself carefully onto the chair I held steady.

"Flattery will get you everywhere. When it comes to cooking I'm like Blanche. I don't want truth; I want magic."

"Cue the paper lanterns."

"A little vino rosso with your kitsch?"

"Please, *por favor, s'il vous plaît*."

We ate in silence for a few seconds. Then Harold spoke. "It tastes even better than it looks." He paused just a minute. "I've been thinking, Geoffry. How come you twigged so fast to the fact that I was gay? I thought my so-called straight façade was pretty convincing."

"It was. But my gaydar is finely tuned to pick up small, almost subliminal clues. Don't embarrass me by asking for details, at least not until I know you better. Does Macy's tell Gimbel's?"

"Okay, I won't. It's just that you are very clued in for a married man."

"You must remember, Harold, that there was a long period in my life, between my first and second marriages, when I was a free agent, a very free agent. But," I couldn't resist a chuckle, "I was redeemed by the love of a good woman."

Harold joined me in a quiet laugh. "I'm truly glad to hear it. What was she like — Elinor? I'm curious about the kind of woman you would marry, and, furthermore, very successfully, it would appear. Unless you would rather not talk about her."

"Not at all. I do not indulge myself in the trappings of grief. Elinor herself would be the first to disapprove of mourning as theatre. To begin with, it was a mixed marriage: we weren't even the same sex. Little joke there. Aside from being beautiful, in that understated WASP way: you know: gorgeous pewter hair worn in a short pageboy; luminous hazel eyes; beautiful skin (In my books no woman can be truly beautiful unless she has good skin.); good, slightly gone-by, lived-in figure, she was easy to live with, for me at least. Without being a crone, or a witch, or a sybil, she was a wise woman, one who wore her wisdom lightly. In a nutshell, she was smart; but I was smarter. If I was wise, she was wiser. We did not tread on one another's toes. It was a good combination.

"She once told me she had always hoped to meet a man she could look up to without having to lie down. Perhaps I wasn't that man, but at the very least I didn't use my car keys to clean my ears. We had our differences. What couple doesn't? And now that she is dead they seem petty and trivial. Fortunately we live from day to day as though we are immortal. On a clear day you can live forever. I told her you can't teach an old dog new tricks. Her reply was, 'Of course you can; it just takes longer.'

"She understood the games and destructive ploys that couples play; and she was wonderful at sending up the whole idea of petty bickering and mind games. She used to say, 'You don't love me anymore; and even if you do, you don't love me enough.' To which I would reply something like, 'I don't like that quilted housecoat. You'd look better in something dark and flowing — like a river.' Then we would laugh and forget what the minor irritation may have been. We did not fight; we didn't have time. As I said, Elinor was a wise woman; she understood that she had married an older man. We may not have been *The Merchant's Tale*, January and May. Rather more November and August, but we understood Homeric battles are for the young. Little did I imagine I would be the one left behind."

Suddenly, I felt a most uncomfortable feeling behind my eyes, an itching sensation that I feared might end in tears. Shakespeare saved the day. For no reason that I could imagine I thought of Desdemona's line: "Mine eyes do itch. / Doth that bode weeping?" To which Emilia replies, "'Tis neither here nor there." It was such an Elinor kind of reply that I smothered the feeling and switched to another subject.

"Elinor was a good mother, and grandmother. She had grandchildren, not toddlers. She had brainwashed her own children into all the accepted values: courtesy to elders, good table manners, the correct use of irregular plurals, a distaste for kitsch, and a pride in country that did not extend to wearing the maple leaf on clothing. Her approach to the endless demands of grandchildren, for whom Granny was seen as a walking cornucopia, was, 'Tell me what you want, and I'll tell you how to get along without it.' She did not advocate grief counselling for dead goldfish and hamsters. And when they were sick she believed that medicine, not laughter, was the best medicine. She was quite a woman, and … You will have to excuse me."

I fled. Elinor herself would have said, "Big boys don't cry." But I did; I had a good bad cry, and felt immensely better for it.

⌒

I walked over to the printer to pick up my invitations and to help restore my equilibrium. I have never been given to fits of weeping, certainly not in front of strangers; and in spite of any chance biological connections I still thought of Harold as a relative stranger. I am sure he too must have felt uncomfortable as he watched me leave the room in tears; but, oddly enough, I found myself minding much less than I would have, say, twenty years ago. Emotional skin thickens with age. What I minded most was not that Harold had seen me weep, but that I had allowed him into the private space that is my grief for Elinor. My feeling for her is my own business, the do not enter sign clearly displayed; but possibly I had shed the tears I ought to have shed at the funeral. Like most Canadians, I am not a professional mourner, able and willing to howl and keen, rend my garments, fling myself about, and generally carry on in a very un-WASP fashion for a few rupees, or dinars or, always acceptable American dollars. And fuck it; it's done!

I was also wryly amused at Harold's surprise at being pegged as a gay man. How had I known? How indeed? To be sure, he was not the least bit, to use a bygone term, "nelly." Rather the opposite. Harold Baldwin would be a formidable opponent in any real disagreement. He had both words and the ability to deploy them; I have no doubt he would lay about him handily with a blunt instrument should the necessity arise. There was definitely an edge, almost too sharp an edge. At the same time I thoroughly enjoyed his verbal dexterity, his ability to seize a trope and run with it.

Only yesterday I had remarked, after turning on the radio for hourly news, that Doo-wop songs must surely be under attack from the Italian Anti-Defamation League.

Harold had laughed. "Does that mean pet stores can no longer sell Guinea pigs?"

"Only if you promise to feed them sauerkraut."

"Which is best cooked in the fall, when there is a Nip in the air."

"Chink in the armour."

"Jig-saw."

"When you take a shower do you have a Wetback?"

"Yes, but I always leave the bathroom Spic and span."

I threw up my hands. "Truce. Besides if He takes His eye off the sparrow for one second we are in deep trouble."

I am almost certain there are straight men out there, aside from composers and lyricists, who know the words to Broadway shows; only I have never met any. Show lyrics remain a kind of litmus test, like rapture over sequins, or shaving your legs unless you race on bicycles. (Athletes claim shaving cuts down on wind resistance. Sure it does, Mary.) Even as these idle thoughts sifted through my mind I understood my gay signifiers were now as out of date as leg-of-mutton sleeves or the farthingale. The gay scene as I knew it has gone the way of the pterodactyl, the Ottoman Empire, hoop skirts, and jello molds. AIDS, gay activism, and what passes for tolerance in Straightland has changed *les règles de jeu*. I remember Bette Davis as a tragedienne, not a camp collection of tics and mannerisms which are fodder for female impersonators. How many times has *Gypsy* been revived. I saw it with Ethel Merman. And who under forty even knows who Ethel Merman is?

When I see young men today, heads shaved, gilded with tattoos, pierced in places that I can see and probably in places I'd rather not see, I wonder what happened to the mauve tie or the green carnation. I approve the greater honesty about matters sexual even as I wonder whether the young men and women, trying to be trendy, ever wonder about the signals their clothes are sending out, anything from "Hi, sailor" to "I fuck on the first date." Like most Anglo-Saxons of my age I feel deprived when my guilty pleasures no longer carry even the faintest suggestion of guilt. Go with the flow. Let it all hang out. Don't worry; be happy. Whatever it is, it's cool. Will young people today even know the illicit thrill of having the family house to yourself for a weekend and inviting a friend over for maybe, just maybe, having sex? The slightly illicit was its own high.

I don't buy into that When-I-was-a-boy bullshit. Things were not better, only different. Would I want to be young again? No. Would I want to be Harold's age again? Not really. What I would really like is to be the age I am with Elinor at my side. "If wishes were horses, beggars would ride," as Mother used to say. She probably still would, given the opportunity. After all, a cliché a day keeps thought at bay.

On the plus side, Harold's being gay, or admitting the same, takes the pressure off me to keep my hairpins in place. I generally do, but could I really be comfortable around someone claiming to be my son who would pass censorious judgement on roughly three quarters of my life as an adult. If I remember correctly, I was around fifteen when I became, as is said in the newspapers, "sexually active," meaning there is at least one other person present. (I have always thought sex must be hard on loners. Unless you have rich fantasies, the act generally involves someone else.) I have been married twice, once for around two years, the second time for five. That leaves forty-eight years for experimenting with "the love that knows no name," which has turned into the political hot potato that doesn't know when to shut up, to mix my metaphor. Whether I would ever feel comfortable enough with Harold to talk freely about past experiences remained an open question. Friendships can suffer from too much candour, just as much as from too little. And no doubt

Harold had areas in his life best left behind drawn curtains. Things have a way of working themselves out. In the meantime, his arrival in my life could not have come at a more opportune time. I have been obliged to think about something other than the hole left by Elinor's death. And for this reason alone I will be forever in debt to Harold Baldwin, whatever his antecedents.

The printer had done a first-rate job on the invitations. The simple message on heavy embossed paper was at once austere and elegant. Elinor might have found them too austere, but this time it was my call. Besides, I knew that once that bunch of free-loaders got a couple of drinks under their respective belts, all traces of austerity and elegance would evaporate in the convivial din. On my way to the printer's, I passed a young lout wearing a tee-shirt that read "Drink 'til you want me." In his case it would take more liquor than my liver was presently capable of processing, but I did admire the sentiment. I hoped Elinor's party would turn into a good, old-style wake: boozy, teary, sentimental, and hugely enjoyable. Elinor was going to go raucously into that good night, and I hoped that all those present would remember the evening as long as their ageing memories continued to function. After all, what better tribute than being remembered.

∽

The day being fine, I walked back to my apartment. Walking allows me to reflect in an unhurried, free-associative way, and these days I had much to think about. To begin with, I had to get in touch with Jane about turning over possession of Elinor's house. I know she chafed over my injunctions; but had it not been for my intervention, she would not be inheriting the property. While Elinor was alive, her children thought of me as a welcome addition to the family. As long as Elinor was married to me they need not concern themselves unduly over her wellbeing. Geoffry was there to cope with an emergency, should it arise. However, once it became clear that Elinor would never leave the hospital, Jane began to cast covetous eyes on her mother's goods and chattels. No longer the resident care-giver, I found myself recast as the importunate outsider ready and perhaps willing to come between Elinor's estate and the claims of her legitimate heirs. Once Jane, and to a lesser extent Gregory, realized that I was not going to do them out of their birthright, they began to wonder how long it would be before I was prepared to stand aside and grant them full access to "the second-best bed" and all that went along with it. Although a part of me wanted to drag my feet out of sheer bitchiness, I understood that their unseemly eagerness to shunt me aside and claim the stuff freed me from any further obligations to pretend we had become family. They could both go fuck themselves and leave me in peace.

The last time I went to the house, my purpose had been to pick up mail and see all was in order. I had not thought of the visit as being my last. Yet were I to go back to the house one more time, before giving Jane the keys, I would wander discon-solately through empty rooms fully aware it was for the last time. This awareness would wring me out. So much good living had been experienced under that roof that I dreaded closing the door once and for all. Were I to turn the house over to Jane without going back, my last visit would not be the "last" visit. And I would be spared the experience of watching THE END appear on the mindscreen of my life with Elinor. Had my arthritic shoulders permitted, I would have patted myself on the back.

Then there was the prospect of the newly discovered Harold Baldwin. Get lost, stepchildren; I now, for better or for worse, have a son of my own. I may not be from Missouri, but I was not about to cast caution to the winds and open up my heart, my life, and perhaps my wallet to a complete stranger. I hoped one day I might feel so inclined. I suppose Harold Baldwin did not qualify as a brand-new son. At best he had arrived slightly shop-soiled, but still serviceable.

So far I liked him, an encouraging start. Had I not found him engaging I don't know how I would have reacted. I was way too old to undergo an *éducation sentimentale*; furthermore, I felt no responsibility for the man. His mother had married her long-term fiancé and passed the baby off as his. Jane had chosen her life, and had it not been for the uncontrollable candour of senile dementia, the connection between Harold and me would have remained hidden. As a result, I was not about to start beating my bony breast and tearing my thinning hair in a theatrical display of paternal feeling I did not feel.

Still, the forecast remained favourable. His being gay meant I would not have to adopt a faux-fake demeanour of heterosexual gravitas. Nor will I be obliged to join the dots; his is a mind that can jump from A to D without making pit stops at B and C. I am fully aware of the bromide that goodness can exist in mediocre minds. ("Be good, sweet maid, and let who will be clever.") but I am not talking about delivering Meals on Wheels or collecting clothing for hurricane victims. When confronted by a real moral choice, say the death penalty or euthanasia on demand, a few gray cells can help greatly in making an informed decision. Harold appeared to have gray cells in abundance.

So far he has not admitted to a predilection for gardening or making his own furniture on a lathe. As much as that mythical figure known as "the next person," I enjoy a well-tended garden or an equally well turned, hand crafted rocker. It is just that those who hoe and plant, sand and wax, are not *ipso facto* imbued with a deep and nurturing wisdom that can raise the most depressed of spirits. My experience has been that most gardeners and woodworkers are likeable airheads who don't know what the hell to do with their spare time.

My sister Mildred loves to garden. She reads seed catalogues the way doctors read *Lancet*. She also bristles when I refer to her as the old hoer; but I have to admit that her brown-eyed Susans, which she resolutely calls rudbeckia, are above reproach. Wait until Mildred learns she has a brand new nephew, confident, as I am sure she is, that her children stand to inherit my estate. After all, having no issue of my own, why would I not leave everything to my nieces and nephews? I should try to capture the moment of disclosure on video. Mildred is given to locking the barn door after the horse has escaped in order to make sure it can't get back inside, so her reaction to Harold is bound to be unpredictable. But all in due course.

Suddenly I was entering the door of my apartment building and nodding a greeting to the doorman. A good wool-gather does pass the time, and it certainly beats going over old grudges, or planning practical jokes, or brooding over elections.

I let myself into the apartment. "The lord and master has returned," I called out by way of greeting.

"With a crust for the starving child, one hopes," replied Harold. To my surprise his voice came not from the master bedroom nor from the dining room. Instead he came to stand at the door of the bedroom I had made into an office.

"I was just moving about," he offered by way of explanation, "seeing how well I could manage by myself on crutches. The sooner I am mobile, the sooner I will be off your hands." He smiled disarmingly. "I hope you don't mind, but I used the phone on your desk to call Toronto. Naturally I used my phone card." Harold went on to explain the friend he had telephoned was making a quick visit to Montreal, driving down tomorrow and returning the following day. He owned a suv, a vehicle large enough to accommodate a tall passenger with cast, and Harold had decided to avail himself of the opportunity.

"In spite of any long faces I may have pulled over meals, there is no urgency for you to leave. Do you think it is wise to operate on your own so soon?"

"I won't have to. I called another friend who lives not far

from me in a ground floor condo. I can stay with him for a while. He is out all day and works long hours. I also have an appointment to see my own doctor, under whose care I would prefer to be. It really is better this way, Geoffry. It may be two or three weeks before the cast comes off, and I don't want to wear out my welcome after so brief an acquaintance."

I threw up my hands. "What can I say. Other than that you're welcome to stay. But you are a grown man. If returning to Toronto suits you best, so be it."

As I stirred the kidney beans in the double boiler and turned the Polish sausages in the pan, I realized that the day after tomorrow would see the departure of Harold, if not for good at least for a while. I would not miss the kitchen patrol, or the cigarettes; but I would miss the presence of another human being in the apartment. Over and above the evident novelty of getting to know a son of whom I had no prior knowledge, his care and feeding obliged me to force my thoughts in directions away from Elinor. With Harold gone, emptiness would flow in to fill the apartment, leaving me to flounder through the days until I managed to reestablish some sort of routine and pretend it was a life.

At the moment I could almost, almost but not quite, envy those who cultivated hobbies. I dislike fishing, so tying my own flies is a non-starter. With my narrow chest I could never be a glass blower, a limitation with which I have come to terms. I have never owned a loom, nor known anyone who did. Never have I been swept with a desire to capture autumn tints, a

Laurentian sunrise, or a covered bridge in acrylics. I quite dislike pottery, which is best left to the professionals. Furthermore, I have reached the age when the urge to shed possessions vastly outweighs the wish to acquire them. Collecting anything is out. Reading, in spite of sanctimonious observations to the contrary, is not a career. Television is at best a diversion. Nor do I listen to recordings of string quartets, eyes closed in rapture, as I work out cello fingerings on my ribcage. The ineluctable truth remains that, for a man of supposed taste and education, those inner resources, which are supposed to nourish and sustain, shrivel and dry up when needed. And Harold, with his cast, his opinions, his half revelations, and his intelligence, had successfully kept the demons of solitude at bay. I was going to miss him more than I cared to admit.

At the same time, I had to remind myself, as my dear old granny used to say, that halitosis is better than no breath at all. Harold still had another forty-eight hours before he headed back to Toronto. Two thousand eight hundred and eighty minutes was scant time to catch up with all those missing years, but it would have to do.

As a gesture of thumbing my nose at life in general, I opened a bottle of chianti, sadly no longer available in a straw covered fiasco, but potable nonetheless. I carried a glass in to Howard, presently reading the newspaper with his cast on a footstool. As of today we had decided to dispense with the services of Nurse Janice and her glum good cheer. Each day she came closer to sharing major revelations about her private life. As I had

—

97

initially suspected, there was an absentee husband, only instead of decamping with her best friend he had been caught pushing drugs and was serving time in jail. There were children about whom she was obviously dying to unburden herself; but I headed her off with a little envelope crackling with bills. Her thanks for the unexpected gratuity were profuse; and in the explosion of "Thank you, Sir; Oh, you shouldn't have; It really is too kind," I managed to guide her through the door, steer her towards the elevator and nudge her out of our lives. Sic transit Janice.

A glass or two of wine on an empty stomach loosens the tongue, as once was said. A drink or two does not so much loosen the tongue as shut down the built-in censor we have all been raised to obey. While Harold did his best to eat most of my admittedly stodgy lunch, he paused to drink wine.

"You know something, Geoffry, in our brief sojourn together I appear to have done most of the talking. You know about my admittedly checkered past, but I know practically nothing about you. You have been married twice, early and late. You are a retired lawyer. And that's about it."

"Would you like me to fall down drunk, like Hoffman in the opera, and tell you of my great loves, all unconsummated?"

Harold laughed, a contagious sound, unlike my laughter which was almost soundless. "I would prefer something along the lines of Don Giovanni and his lists, a thousand and three in Spain alone. I'm way too old to be shocked, and with two wives your straight credentials are impeccable. So fill in some of the gaps."

It was my turn to laugh. "Listen, kid, you're heading home in forty-eight hours. That gives me almost time, given that we have to eat and sleep, to get me as far as forty. So perhaps I had better condense. I have been in love, or what I thought was love, many times. Many, many times. And lots and lots of rehearsals. If there is one thing I have learned, one bit of fatherly wisdom worth passing on to the next generation — that's you, by the way — it is that one learns to love, really to love, over the period of a lifetime. I was young once, believe it or not; and I confused — you will excuse my candour — a stiff prick with the love of my life. I was wrong. Just as experience makes you a better lawyer, or teacher, or doctor, so one learns to love." I couldn't resist a laugh like a giggle. "I'm not talking about those techniques you learn from books and videos: erotic massage with exotic oils, still newer uses for the electric toothbrush, concentrating on last night's pot roast so you can last longer. In other words, the mechanics of intercourse, that which used to be called fucking. Aren't you taking notes? I am moving to the far side of pedantic."

Harold mimed sitting up straight and paying attention. "I don't have to. I'm riveted. Please continue."

"There's not much more to tell. My first, supposedly roman- tic loves were callow and narcissistic. I observed myself being in love and gave myself little pats on the back for being so sensitive and caring. The first bump in the road and it was over. Then on to the next manifestation of sensual sensitivity, the perfect mix of heaven and earth, with particular emphasis

—

on the earth part. Then a cross word, an inflated misunderstanding, an imaginary slight — and it was time to go out on the prowl."

I paused for a large swallow of chianti. "I was never in love with Elinor. I mean 'in love' after the manner of Romeo and Juliet, Héloise and Abélard, Hero and Léander; the list goes on. But I loved her in a way I have never loved anyone before. She was my last, true love. And when she died I closed the book."

Harold placed his knife and fork together, the way he had been taught as a child. "I am prepared to challenge that last assumption. There is more than one kind of love. It really ought to be a plural noun. Love for family, friends, pets — even maybe, some day, for a long-lost, newly-discovered son."

"That," I said with a shrug and a rearranging of the mouth that did not quite mature into a smile, "remains to be seen."

# 6

*M*embers of the younger generation today use an expression I particularly enjoy. They "hang out" with their friends. The term suggests a relaxed, unstructured way of spending time together. A "visit" strikes me as formal and borderline dreary, with its overtones of hospital rooms and residences for the aged. At best the word conjures up a time when calling cards were ritually placed in sliver trays, an era of formal parlours where people sat stiffly on small, uncomfortable chairs and made equally small talk. "To spend quality time" with someone seems both pretentious and condescending, almost as though the one spending the quality time were also bestowing grace with his mere presence. But hanging out can encompass a number of pleasant, undemanding activities, such as having a drink, watching TV, playing cards, sending out for pizza, or sharing the newspaper. I realize now that what I already miss about my life with Elinor, and will continue to regret, is quite simply hanging out together.

For the next two days Harold and I hung out. We watched TV, had drinks, and sent out for barbequed chicken. Harold did not much care for playing cards; and, to be perfectly candid, neither do I. We did not have to share the newspaper as I subscribe to two. Between us we were able to manage a shower. I duct-taped a plastic garbage bag over his cast and helped him, still wearing a bathrobe, into the tub. From behind the curtain he handed me the robe. I felt surprisingly shy about seeing him naked. God knows, I have seen plenty of bare-assed bucks in my time, but I belong to the generation for whom nudity is strongly sexual. I suppose it is a holdover from an earlier time, when the air was clean and sex was dirty — and a hell of a lot more fun.

With freshly shampooed hair and a shave, Harold admitted to feeling almost human. While we listened to the morning programs on CBC he helped me slide invitations into envelopes, seal, and stamp them. I took the invitations directly to the post office, rollerskated through the supermarket, and took a taxi home with my groceries, unwilling to be away from the apartment any longer than necessary. Eventually I was to realize these two days when I had my newly discovered son to myself were to be cherished, to be taken out and examined the way one venerates certain personal treasures ordinarily tucked away in a cabinet or a drawer.

What I remember above all else was that Harold made me

laugh. I will not go so far as to say he is a funny man, as humour is at once intensely personal and quirky. Like soft cheese, humour does not travel well. How many times have Canadians sat stony-faced while British comics knocked themselves out to be amusing. Newfie jokes fail to amuse Americans, and a great many Canadians it must be admitted. I have been told the French tell jokes about Belgians, the Danes about Swedes, and the Spanish about the Portuguese. Although I have thus far been spared these ethnic sallies, would I double up in mirth? I doubt it.

Yet Harold managed to find a ridiculous side to everyday events, and I found myself laughing in agreement. "Why do you suppose," he asked of a TV commercial, "that people on vacation tend to lose their travellers' cheques on the beach or the golf course? If there are two places in the world where one is less likely to need cash than on the links or the shore I'd like to know them."

On another occasion he asked, "Have you ever really seen someone laughing all the way to the bank? I never have. Banks are daunting rather than hilarious, far more likely to induce tears than mirth; but that image is cast in concrete."

Over tea one afternoon we discussed our favourite movie clichés. I volunteered the bartender carefully wiping the inside of a glass while he listens to a morose detective who is still in love with his ex-wife. Harold suggested two: the neon sign blinking outside the window of a seedy hotel room, and a police car chase during which a fruit stand is sent flying. We agreed that stolen clothes always seem to fit, and dark glasses make the wearer invisible.

How corny and inconsequential it all seems now, not even worth remembering. What I recall most of all is the pleasure I took in laughing, a pleasure I had not enjoyed since Elinor went into the hospital. Our lives had been filled with laughter, and I missed it more than I would have thought possible. Harold had made me laugh, and I was indebted.

During those brief forty-eight hours Harold and I did nothing of any great interest. His movement was still greatly curtailed by the cast. We spoke of mundane matters, unable and unwilling to solve the problems of the world. The closest we came to a disagreement was over the major matter of Jean Harlow as opposed to Mae West. One afternoon we watched *Bombshell* and *I'm No Angel*, both of which I happen to have on VHS, or "Very High Sissy," as a friend once called my video collection. I countered by observing something about the pot and the kettle, and that anyone who lived in an apartment that was so UHF (Ultra High Fag) he could barely get through the door for curtains, tchotchkes, and crap, was in no position to cast the first bibelot. We continued in this vein for a while, until he became so angry he gave me a piece.

Harold had never seen either film, hardly surprising considering they both came out in 1933 before either of us was born. I am not given to gushing enthusiasms over show biz celebrities. Maybe this reluctance to applaud is due to one too many evenings during my fauve period spent on gin and Judy Garland records, scotch and Frank Sinatra records, or warm chablis and show tunes. But I confess a special fondness for the snap, crackle, and pop of Jean Harlow, whose energy lit up the screen in a regrettably few comedies before she died an untimely death when I was only three. How pointless and foolish and refreshing it was to get into an argument over two sex symbols, both dead, and now immortalized as gay icons.

"You have to realize, Harold, that when you have seen as many Mae West impersonators as I have over the course of a long lifetime, it's hard to take the real thing seriously."

"But, don't you see, the fact that so many people do take her off means she is a true cultural icon. Nobody does Jean Harlow impersonations."

"That's easy to explain. She is inimitable. Furthermore, she is an actress, not a nightclub act. Had she lived, she would have become a true actress, a comédienne as the French call actors who do not specialize in heavy tragedy. I grant you, North Americans have always admired actors who can make them cry more than those who make them laugh. It is our great cultural deficiency. Wait! I haven't finished — and you have to defer to my greater age. I am not denigrating Mae; she is truly droll. But she is funny after the manner of a stand-up comic. There is one persona she always plays, and you wait for the famous lines. 'Why don't you come up sometime, and see me? It's not the men in your life but the life in your men. I used to be white as snow, and then I drifted.' Harlow, on the other hand, works from a script and creates a character. And if you don't believe me watch *Dinner at Eight*. Her scenes with Wallace Beery are among the best on film. Now it's your turn."

Harold inclined his head. "All you say is true, but everyone from Patagonia to Vladivostok knows Mae West. Jean Harlow is just another bygone star."

"Them's fightin' words, and luckily for you it's part of my code never to strike a man wearing a cast. Jean Harlow died young, with only a few really good films to her credit. Mae West made a movie when she was well over eighty. Sadly, she still believed the hype and thought of herself as a sex goddess, when she could barely get out of a chair. Longevity and a talent for self-promotion do not necessarily add up to acting. Being a personality, yes. But once you have created this instantly recognizable personality you are trapped inside it, like that character in the Pirandello play. *Henry IV* I think."

"You're right. I have to say that, or I won't get any dinner. But, pardon my asking, what precisely are we arguing about?"

Suddenly we were both convulsed with laughter.

Harold was the first to speak. "Do you have a tape of *Dinner at Eight*?"

"It just so happens I do. Elinor loved Jean Harlow. I also have a tape of *My Little Chickadee*, Mae playing off against W.C. Fields, perhaps the only leading man who could steal a scene from her. The war of personalities. She disliked his drinking, and he called her a plumber's idea of Cleopatra. They disliked one another and made a marvellous movie. Do you happen to have any plans for this evening?"

Harold smiled broadly. "None at the moment, outside of the silver screen. Come to think of it, black and white movies do look silver from a distance."

"I'd better slide the chops into the oven and molest the lettuce. Can you spare me?"

"With difficulty. But I'll catch up on back issues of *The New Yorker*. I see it's addressed to Elinor."

"True enough. I subscribed to *The Economist*, but we both pounced on *The New Yorker*. As I grow older I want to be diverted, not improved."

That was a pretty good exit line, and I went into the kitchen to begin preparing dinner. First of all, I poured myself a scotch. Drinking and driving may not mix, but drinking and cooking certainly do, at least in the School of G. Chadwick Cuisine.

Dinner eaten, or rather dealt with, Harold and I settled down to watch more old movies. *Dinner at Eight* finds Jean Harlow playing the ultimate bimbo, and the movie concludes with Canada's own Marie Dressler bringing off the greatest double-take on film. A well corseted Mae West sashayed her way through *My Little Chickadee* and did her best to upstage W.C. Fields, possibly the only droll drunk on screen. In the best inside joke tradition each ends the film with the other's signature line. Virtue does not triumph; but, then again, did it ever? Finally, dazed by black and white images and too besotted to sleep, we watched *The Great Lie*, the woman's film that whacks all others into the outfield. Bette Davis, trying to be sweet and good, undertakes Mary Astor's baby because the man they both love is presumed dead. Of course he turns up; and Mary Astor, playing what should have been the Bette Davis role, turns nasty and threatens to reclaim her child. On top of everything else she is a concert pianist, meaning Russian romantic. From time to time she gets very angry at the keyboard. Like all women's movies it ends happily unhappily. I must have dropped off just about the time George Brent, everyman as leading man, turns up, still presumably married to Mary Astor. What I do remember is the women's hair: Mary Astor in a short crop that would not look out of place on today's metrosexual and Bette Davis getting maximum mileage from a shoulder length pageboy, much tossed about.

I roused myself just long enough to go to bed; I presume Harold did the same.

The following morning found me a bit bleary-eyed from our orgy of movies; but I still managed to bring off Eggs Benedict, the closest one gets to sin at breakfast. The Hollandaise sauce came from a jar, I have to confess; but even so Eggs B. are a huge fiddle. I cooked two apiece, but Harold ended up eating three as I had little appetite. Another ending loomed; or, to make a stab at Cheerful Charlie optimism, I was about to undertake a new beginning. I would have much preferred an old beginning, one going back to meeting Elinor. Much as I tried to dispel a bad attack of the glums, I could only offer minimal conversation. Fortunately the second newspaper and the third Egg Benedict occupied Harold's attention, and he appeared not to notice my reticence.

He glanced at his watch. "Guess I had better think about pulling self together. My friend should be here in about twenty minutes."

"I'll help you get organized," I volunteered. "I'll clear away the remains of breakfast after you've gone."

❧

It was with more genuine regret I would have thought possible that I stood on the sidewalk outside my apartment building watching Harold drive away. I could almost have wished the pathetic fallacy to kick in by providing a wet, dreary day to match my frame of mind. Instead the morning, overcast but still bright, glowed with the particular autumn light that turns yellow leaves to gold, dull brown to amber. By now the soft maples had shed their flamboyant crimson, just as well as I had no wish to be cheered.

Harold's friend, his broad, pleasant face innocent of intelligence, struck me as one of those men born to be perpetually accommodating. He was the man painting the inside of the swimming pool while the other helpers sat in deck chairs drinking beer. He would find himself pinch-hitting at parties, carving the ham, pouring the wine, drying the dishes. They also wait who only stand and serve.

Between us, we got Harold, whom I had helped dress in a pair of my old gym shorts with legs wide enough to go on over the cast, down the elevator and to the car. I had packed his suitcase, which went into the trunk. Before easing himself into the passenger seat, pushed back as far as it would go, Harold turned towards me for a typically Canadian leave-taking, terse to the point of near silence.

"Well, I guess this is it, for the time being. I'll call when I get to Toronto."

"Please do."

"I can't thank you enough for everything you have done."

"A couple of meals and some free TV? The least I could do after fifty years. Will you be coming back to Montreal?"

"Just as soon as I can walk without a cane." He smiled a wan smile. "Well, I guess it's time to go."

At that point Harold and I might, just might, have embraced, stiffly of course as we were in the street. However, crutches and a cast do not permit spontaneous gestures. Instead, Harold handed me his crutches and lowered himself into the seat.

"Here, I'll take those," said the obliging friend.

"Do not be a stranger," was my parting shot as the car pulled away from the curb. My reluctance to see him go sprang from more than any newly discovered family connection. For a brief, few days I had been forced to think about someone other than myself. Not that I failed to think of Elinor; her absence remained a constant presence, but I was diverted by the novelty of Harold, both the who and the what. His departure threw me back on myself, leaving me almost more solitary than had he never come into my life. I felt bloody-minded; and, were I to be perfectly honest, not always a sound policy, I would have to admit to rather enjoying myself. Raised to believe that not being happy showed a lamentable want of character, I took perverse enjoyment in feeling miserable. Let other saps count their goddamned blessings.

As I entered the apartment I could hear the telephone ringing. I have voice mail, and many years have passed since I last hurried to answer the phone. The ring continued, allowing me ample time to go into the alcove.

"Hello?" I said sharply, just before the answering tape kicked in.

"I hope you weren't in the shower or on the pot," said Larry in his slightly nasal voice, "but I really wanted to catch you."

"No, I'm up and about: shaved, showered, and wearing my designer hair shirt. What's up?"

"Can you believe? Last night I woke up in a strange bed. Mine!"

"It's age, kiddo. You can't teach an old dog to turn new tricks. What's on your mind?"

"Last time we spoke I threatened to come to Montreal, to raise your flagging spirits and divert you with my charismatic presence; and it's all happening. Desmond — that's my gentleman caller — needs to do some research at one of the McGill libraries for a paper he's been invited to give at a conference. That's when a bunch of academics get together and bore each other to death. So we're bumping up our projected visit to Montreal. In fact, we fly in this afternoon."

"Should I alert the press, the Quebec Provincial Police, the gay village?"

"That will not be necessary. And it is only your emotionally fragile state that prevents me from suggesting you fuck off."

"Your consideration overwhelms me."

"Are you free for dinner tonight?"

"As a matter of fact, yes."

"Can we come by for a drink? We'll take you to dinner, but it cuts down on the overhead if we drink your liquor first."

"I'll lay on a few kegs. Say around six-thirty to seven?"

"Sounds good. If we encounter a major mishap I'll call."

As I replaced the receiver I knew that whatever direction, possibly bizarre and unforseen, the evening might take, I would not have time to indulge myself in misery. Nor was I about to start counting those blessings. With Larry it pays to begin from a position of strict neutrality and hope for the best.

I went into my own bedroom, redolent of stale cigarettes, to change the bed. I have a cleaning woman, a cheerful Mexican lady named, like every cleaning woman the world over, Maria. I have a feeling her landed immigrant status is a bit dicey, but I ask no questions. She is presently in Mexico, Oaxaca I believe, where her daughter is about to have twins. I have always thought of Mexico as a land of Aztec pyramids, silver and turquoise jewellery, and tourists with the trots. I am sure the country can provide pre-natal ultrasound; but the idea jars my easy perceptions of fiestas, piñatas, cheap tequila, and daredevil drivers. Someday I may visit and find out for myself. In the meantime I hope Maria will be allowed back into the country. I will gladly vouch for the fact that she is not about to sabotage the St. Lawrence Seaway or blow up the Sun Life Building, because I sure as hell do not want to break in another cleaning woman. Elinor was wonderful at dealing with chars; she managed to strike just the right balance between solicitude over their endless family problems and a gentle but firm insistence that they vacuum under the bed. Yet another reason to miss her. The list grows longer.

Before going to work, I sprayed the room with one of those pressurized cans that calls itself an air freshener. These blasts of chemical scent do not freshen the air but they do help to overpower the prevailing odour. After several squirts from the nozzle the room did not smell like a country garden, as promised. Rather, it smelled like a stuffy bedroom in which a sweet, pungent odour battled for supremacy with that of stale cigarettes. In defiance of the air conditioning, I opened the window for a refreshing blast of urban smog, at that moment the lesser of two evils.

Tossing the pillows onto the floor, I stripped the bed. In spite of the reek I looked forward to regaining my own box spring and mattress. It was only when I picked up the pillows to shake them free of the cases that I discovered the burn. A hole the size of a dime, charred around the edges, pierced its way through the pillow case, the second protective case, and the fabric of the pillow itself, so that feathers escaped through the opening.

For a moment I stared in disbelief. How would the pillow case come to display a burned hole unless Harold had been smoking in bed. How indeed? Had I not made perfectly clear that there was to be no smoking in bed? What really galled me is that, having welcomed him into my home, I had not asked him to refrain from smoking — except in bed. No one, not even the most addicted smoker, would consider my request unreasonable. I realized that getting onto his feet and into the bathroom required effort. Yet I was prepared to live with the lingering odour, just so long as he did not present a fire hazard.

A further question made its importunate presence felt. Harold must have known about the burn. If there is one smell more rank than that of stale butts, it is that of singed feathers. Why had he not mentioned the damaged pillow? Had he forgotten, in the confusion of departure? Or had he simply decided to say nothing?

Pillows are easily replaced. Trust is not. As I pushed the sheets into the washing machine I realized he must have drowned his butts in the glass of ice water I kept beside his bed. Then when he went to pee he flushed the evidence away. Perhaps it was just as well I had made the discovery after Harold had left. I would like to simmer down before broaching the subject. I could hardly send him to his room, or ground him weekends, or withhold his allowance. But I could let him know I was displeased; and furthermore, he would damn well pay for replacing the pillow.

# 7

have known Larry longer than anyone else in my Rolodex, exception made for my Mother and sister; but I still find it difficult to decide whether he is a friend or a burden. To be sure, age has slowed him down somewhat; but Larry in low gear is like anyone else in overdrive. Sober, a condition that lasts until his first drink of the day, he has more energy than a room full of high school students. Around six p.m. he dives into the gin, his beverage of choice, and begins a transformation that would cause Dr. Jekyll and Mr. Hyde to shake their heads in astonishment. Gin unleashes his formidable energy; it also shuts down his judgement, his ability to assess a situation and take the more prudent course. He has survived more hangovers, quarrelled with more lovers, turned more tricks, and narrowly avoided more brushes with the law than any other ten people I know.

Luckily for me, I came to realize I must not be sucked into his slipstream. Facing clients after a night of drinking and sex with strangers is no way to build a career, and I began to limit our outings to drinks and dinner. For the shank of the evening he was on his own; we each climbed into taxis going in different directions, mine home, his to the bars and baths.

Larry's protective colouring has saved his hide on more than one occasion. Small and neat, with bland, unremarkable WASP looks, he always dressed conservatively. A dark suit, blue shirt, striped tie, and oxfords can take you almost everywhere, from Government House, where all the men are similarly attired, to a seedy gay bar where a tie has the charm of novelty. A striped tie also helps when one is stopped by the police at four a.m. in a disreputable part of town. ("Goodness me, Officer, the cab driver must have taken me to the wrong address.") Larry was born with the proverbial silver spoon in his mouth, and I suspect a row of lucky horse shoes hung suspended over his crib.

What could only be described as a fast and loose lifestyle has taken a toll on his face. Unremarkable features have collapsed into wrinkles, an apple left too long in the sun; however, he has kept his figure. The last time I saw Larry, about a year ago, I found him looking suspiciously taut. Tactfully refraining from any questions about nips and tucks, I merely observed he was looking well. He smiled a sly smile, and the movement of skin on cheek suggested a little touch of scalpel. And why not? Elinor used to say I was ageing well, which I took to mean I had not yet begun to resemble the mummy of Ramses II, although one day I will.

What gives me an advantage over Larry is that I really do not care about my ageing appearance. Let the wrinkles, pouches, dewlaps do their worst. Having retired from the sexual arena, I am no longer out to entice. Mere survival will do very nicely, thank you. My marriage did not exactly put a strain on my relationship with Larry; we have known each other too long. But it did place me *hors de combat* and no longer available for protracted cocktail hours and boozy dinners, after which I poured myself into a cab to go home, while Larry skipped off to do the town.

I hoped the presence of a new lover might impose a little decorum on the evening ahead. To watch Larry charge down the hall towards my apartment hinted at the reverse.

"I hope we're not late, precious treasure, but we had a couple of drinks at the hotel."

Were I to believe Larry ever had "a couple of drinks," meaning two, I would also believe in the Tooth Fairy, the Easter Bunny, Santa Claus, caring workplaces, and gentle laxatives.

"Welcome to my humble home. Hello Desmond, I'm Geoffry Chadwick."

Like a heat-seeking missile Larry headed straight for the bar. "Is it really Bombay gin, or did you make it in the bathtub and siphon it into the bottle?"

Ignoring Larry, busy with a tumbler and ice cubes, I shook hands with Desmond Langley and invited him in. My first impression, the one the business columnists claim is the important one, was favourable. Were I to have telephoned central casting and asked for a professor I might well have ended up with a Desmond Langley clone. From his wire-rimmed glasses, to his neatly trimmed beard, longish hair, tattersall shirt, hand-loomed tie, corduroy jacket, chinos, and loafers, he was, in his way, perfect. He also impressed me as being a gentleman.

"What will you drink, Desmond?" I asked, Larry having by now splashed some gin over ice cubes and added a dash of French vermouth, a martini by ear.

"Scotch, please — and a little water. No ice."

I poured two scotches, and in short order we were all out-fitted with a glass.

"What were you drinking earlier?" I asked Larry, forewarned being forearmed.

"Gin and tonic. But enough already. All that fluid makes you want to pee."

"You know how to find the loo." I turned to Desmond, who was maintaining a tactful silence until Larry simmered down. "Where would you like to eat?"

"I'm willing to be guided," he replied, his vowels short, his consonants crisp. "I know Montreal is famous for restaurants."

"He's big on ethnic," blurted out Larry. "All the parts of the animal we make into pet food spiced and simmered and served over brown rice. Awful! One longs for a chop or a cutlet, with a potato and veg."

"How about Italian?" I suggested. "That's small 'e' ethnic." I wanted to get the restaurant question cleared up before Larry became too drunk to eat. Once he dived into the martinis it was fasten-your-seatbelt time. I was also a bit concerned about my own tolerance for Larry drunk. How many evenings have I seen sabotaged by too many drinks. Youth has resilience; middle age offers a degree of tolerance. But I was neither young nor middle aged. Even buying into the happy-face slogan that seventy is the new sixty, I had passed the age for tolerating stupid drunks.

"You are a teacher, rather a professor?" I said to Desmond, giving him an opening I hoped he might take.

"Yes, but I'm on sabbatical this term. I'm working on a book."

"About what?"

"In a nutshell, how the English language evolved from Chaucer to Shakespeare."

"Does it concentrate on linguistics or literature?"

"Both. It's difficult to separate the two."

"Bo-ring!" exclaimed Larry. "I'm going to wait for the movie. I'm also going to have another mart — with your permission. I feel like getting really shitfaced."

"You passed shitfaced about ten miles back," I suggested. "Are you going to spoil another evening by getting stinko?"

"The earth is full, Chadwick. Go home." Upon which he went to the bar for another tumbler of gin. I was getting the feeling of déjà-vu all over again. However, the claims of good manners, the obligation to remain civil in front of a stranger who was also my guest, saved Larry from the retort that lurked just behind my teeth. Why hadn't I lied and said I was busy. There are far worse things than being alone. Ingenuously, I had hoped the presence of a new friend, lover, whatever would impose some decorum. Wrong.

"Have you always taught at the university level?" I asked to get the conversation back on track.

"No, not always. When I was a graduate student, and chronically short of funds, I supply taught in Toronto schools. My trial-by-fire, as it were." He laughed quietly. "The prospect of facing a room full of freshmen fades beside the sheer terror of a high school class turned loose on the supply teacher. I was told on more than one occasion that things in the schools aren't what they used to be. My feeling is that they are exactly what they used to be, and that is precisely the problem."

"Chadwick, stop trying to draw him out. That is unless you're dying to know how French words found their way into Middle English."

Larry's "couple of drinks" must have been quite a few. Larry belongs to the generation that believes that a good time presupposes getting drunk. Going to the opera? Wagner sounds better if you're pissed. Off to the theatre? *Hamlet* has more meaning if you're sloshed. Tickets for the ballet? Who can sit through *Swan Lake* sober? And who can manage a symphony concert, all those concertos and symphonies, and overtures, without doubles, or even triples, at intermission.

As is said today: Been there. Done that.

With a loud, sucking noise Larry drained his glass and put it down on the table with a determined thud.

"Do you know the two biggest Polish lies?" he demanded.

"I realize I am supposed to say no."

"One: Your cheque is in my mouth. Two: I'm not going to come in your mail." Heaving himself to his feet, he went in search of more drink.

"Please, help yourself," I could not resist saying. Age does not always guarantee maturity.

To my surprise, Desmond stood and went to stand beside Larry at the bar. He spoke low, but his whisper carried. "Larry, you've had enough, more than enough. Please don't spoil another evening by getting drunk."

"I'm not spoiling anything. You and Geoffry obviously have plenty to talk about. I'll just sit quiet and enjoy my drink. What's the harm in that?"

Desmond did not reply, but he gave Larry a laser look and returned to his chair. Drink replenished, Larry sat; and for a few moments it appeared as if he intended to maintain his vow of silence.

"Desmond," I began, "I know this is one of those dumb questions. You know: 'You're from Los Angeles. I know some-one in L.A. Do you happen to know …?' But, here goes. In your years as a supply teacher did you happen to run into a Harold Baldwin?"

Desmond hesitated a moment before speaking. "Could he have called himself Harry Baldwin?"

"I'm not sure. He may well have. He's not someone I know well, a friend of a friend. He called me recently while in town and we had lunch. I must admit I quite liked him. He told me he had been a teacher, and I thought perhaps you might have met him professionally."

"If we are talking of the same man," began Desmond, "I didn't really know him, but I knew of him. Is he a friend of yours?"

"Not really. I scarcely know him. But I would be interested in anything that adds dimension to the picture."

Before Desmond could speak, the telephone rang. I went into the bedroom to answer.

"Geoffry, it's me. It is I, Harold, safe and sound in Toronto."

"How was the drive? Tiring?"

"A bit. Fortunately there wasn't much traffic, at least not until after Kingston. We stopped only twice, for a pee and a snack. As I told you, I'm staying with a friend."

"Needless to say I'm relieved to hear you have arrived in one piece."

"I can't thank you enough for all you did. When this break heals and I'm mobile again, I'd like to come for a visit."

"That would be good. If your ankle is sufficiently healed you might want to come to my party. Even if you didn't know Elinor it will give you an excuse. I may have somebody staying with me, so I can't guarantee you a bed here."

"That's okay. I never did get to use that hotel reservation."

"Harold, I won't draw this out as I have friends here. But stay in touch. What is your present number?"

I jotted down seven digits which had a 416 area code, meaning central Toronto.

"I won't keep you," concluded Harold. "Back to your guests, and I'll call in a couple of days. So long — and thanks for everything."

As I returned to my guests I decided to keep Harold's true identity to myself, at least for a while. A secret does wonders for the self-esteem. How many almost eighty-year-olds have a secret that is not tinged around with guilt. If I harboured a regret it was that Elinor would never know about my youthful indiscretion. How she would have laughed, and then gone about the business of absorbing Harold into the family. I was prepared to move more slowly; I already had to digest his disregard of my no smoking request.

As I reentered the living room and read the body language, I suspected there had been a few stern words during my absence. Larry looked abashed, as abashed as Larry is capable of looking, while Desmond sat tall in his chair. I assumed the riot act had just been read. My arrival broke the tension, and I sat.

Desmond was quick to pick up the thread of our conversation. "You were asking about Harry — Harold Baldwin. Can I speak candidly?"

"By all means, I would regret anything else."

"If we are talking about the same man, what I have to report is not favourable. He has a reputation for being very hard on his students. He was a good teacher, no doubt about that; but he terrorized his pupils with sarcasm, low grades, detentions. I also heard he made free with a ruler, or a book, or whatever was handy — never enough to merit censure by the school board, but word got around. Finally he was called onto the carpet. I never learned how it turned out, but the following year he quit teaching."

At a loss for an appropriate comment I went for a quip. "You know what they say about Aspirin: 'Keep away from children.' Good advice for a teacher, even if you don't have a headache."

Desmond laughed on cue. "There's more to the tale, if you are interested."

"Indeed I am," I replied, concealing my dismay with ersatz enthusiasm. "Gossip makes the world go round."

"There was a further rumour," began Desmond; placing his hands on his thighs he leaned forward slightly, "that he beat up on his wife and children. I never heard the whole story, mind you; but she did file for divorce, the year he left teaching, last year as a matter of fact. By then I was at the university, and I only heard of Harry through the grapevine. He was the kind of man who gets himself talked about."

A sudden, loud snore interrupted the narrative; and we both turned to see Larry passed out in his chair.

"There goes the neighbourhood," I observed, "and the evening. From past experience I know we can deal with the situation in one of several ways. We can try to sober him up and hope he makes it through dinner. To be perfectly candid, I'm not ready to risk a restaurant with Larry drunk and comatose. We can put him to bed here, meaning I will have to cope with him, cross and hungover, in the a.m. There was a time when my friendship would have risen to the challenge, but no longer. Since Elinor died I have ceased to be a good sport. Third, you can take him back to the hotel, dump him, and go out for dinner. Lastly, you can leave him be and we can telephone for something to eat. Not much fun on a visit to Montreal, but Larry has always been an unguided missile."

Desmond shook his head slowly from side to side. "Too bad he's such a dumb drinker. Sober, he's a completely different man, kind and amusing. But I'm afraid I'm running out of patience. I'm in the process of building a career, and I have neither the time nor the energy for a companion who goes to bed drunk most nights."

"I sympathize with you, and I'm sorry, truly sorry. It would please me more than you realize to see Larry in a stable relationship, but you are not the Red Cross."

"You're right. And I think the best option is to take him back to the hotel. We had a large lunch, and I'm not particularly hungry. I'll have room service send something up. Sorry about this. We had intended taking you out."

I held up my hands, palms out. "Not to worry. To be perfectly candid, I'm still a bit shakey these days. Had the evening proceeded smoothly I would have enjoyed going out. But under the circumstances I really would prefer to stay home. Shall I call a cab?"

While I telephoned, Desmond shook Larry awake.

"Chadwick," he began, "did you know that oral sex is better than written?"

"I had heard."

"And," he continued as he struggled back to consciousness, "it's better to be pissed off than on!"

"And to think you kiss your mother with that mouth. Are you up to making it downstairs? A cab is on the way."

"I thought we were going out to dinner."

"There's been a change of plans. Desmond is taking you back to the hotel."

Larry sat up straight. "I don't want to go back to the fucking hotel. I want to have dinner!"

"You'll have dinner at the hotel. I'm feeling a bit done in, and I'd prefer to stay home."

"No way. We're going out to dinner — and you're coming along!"

"No, no, you go along with Desmond."

"No! No! No! Yourself! We're going out — for dinner — after I've had another martini."

"Larry," I said, "listen to me carefully because I'm only going to say this once. You are going to leave — now — with Desmond. If you don't I'm going to slap you so hard you'll be in traction until Easter. Do I make myself clear?"

"I guess you do at that." Larry rose unsteadily to his feet. "You know something, Chadwick? Marriage has turned you into a real drag. You used to be as camp as a row of tents. Now you're more boring than a goddamn federal budget."

"All the more reason not to take me out to dinner. Next time, if there is a next time, let's aim for lunch. I no longer can nor wish to drink the night away."

The phone rang to announce the cab waited at the door. As Desmond steered Larry out the door he whispered that he would call tomorrow. I nodded, and they left.

∽

I really did not want to go out for dinner for any number of reasons, of which two were paramount. First, I was well and truly fed up with Larry, not just because of his behaviour this evening but because of similar conduct, or misconduct, over a period of many years. Larry and I are of an age; and if he is still knocking himself out with too many martinis then he will never know better. I grew up surrounded by stupid drunks, way back before drugs became the escape of choice. During what I like to think of as my "fauve" period I had more than my share of evenings fuelled by distilled grape and grain. But that was then. I no longer find it amusing to feel drunk, to enjoy the sensation of extreme sophistication with absolutely nothing intelligible to say. To drive while drunk (So many pedestrians; so little time) is no longer an option. Call it ageing; call it judgement, common sense, maturity, or the buzzword du jour, I have reached a point in my life when stupid, irresponsible, willful behaviour remains just that. I no longer excuse it in myself just as I refuse unapologetically never to tolerate it in others.

I did not expect or even want, what passes for sympathy from Larry. What I would really have liked was no more than a companionable evening, a couple of drinks, a few laughs, some conversation over food, nothing unreasonable or untoward. But his narcissistic self-absorption is incorruptible, so to hell with him!

Even were Larry to have been, for him anyway, solicitous about my widowerhood, if such a word exists, I would have steered him away from the subject. Other people's condolences are a heavy burden to bear; one ends up bending over backwards to reassure the person bearing a long face that you are soldiering on. Like sick room visitors, those who console the desolate usually exact a toll; the invalid or mourner is left gasping from the effort of promoting the idea that all is well. Compassion, like criticism, is better to give than to receive.

I am chary of offering sympathy myself, at least face to face. Flowers usually say what needs to be said better than I can; but I admit to never using those dire sympathy cards offered by florists: "With Deepest Sympathy" in that tedious gothic script that has to be decoded one letter at a time. And always the nagging suspicion that your flowers, regardless of cost, are the coward's way out. And if big boys do cry, in spite of childhood injunctions, it is usually over dead pets, damaged sports cars, or sports trophies one failed to win. Big boys do not cry at funerals.

A second, more pressing reason for not wanting to go out arose from Desmond's casual remarks about Harold or Harry Baldwin. Desmond had managed to make my newly discovered son sound like a proper son-of-a-bitch, and I found the allegations profoundly disturbing. True, there remained the off-chance

that we had not been talking about the same person, but that
sounded like the proverbial last straw. Were I to make allowances
for his uneasy marital status and presently unemployed state,
both or either of which might well cause the ubiquitous happy
face to slide into a frown, I found it difficult to countenance
what sounded like frankly ungentlemanly behaviour. Hardly
had I begun to grow used to the idea of a mature son, furthermore one I found every inclination to like, when a chance
question revealed him to be quite possibly a proper little shit.
Once again I found myself sharply reminded of his ignoring
my strict injunction against smoking in bed.

*Quo vadis?* Possibly the best course of action would be to
ignore what Desmond had disclosed and to carry on with business as usual. Easier said then done. The bee was trapped in the
bonnet; Pandora's box stood open, and I knew perfectly well
I could not ignore what Desmond had told me, even more so
as Desmond had no particular ax to grind. He did not know
Harold and spoke only on hearsay. I felt both dismayed and
perplexed, and I most certainly did not wish to hold up my
end of the conversation during dinner, preoccupied as I was
over whether this unwelcome discovery would compromise
the budding friendship with my son. Moreover, I had brought
up the subject of Harold. If, as the poet says, "A little learning
is a dangerous thing," how much more toxic is only a little
knowledge.

I scrambled some eggs, then turned on the TV. Fred Astaire
and Elinor Powell and George Murphy were all tapping busily

away, rather more than one could wish for in a single movie. After a while I went to bed, not to sleep but to brood in a more comfortable position. After a while I must have fallen asleep, as I grew slowly aware of having emerged from a chaotic dream. I do not remember what it was; and if I did, I would not tell. Whenever someone tells me about an unusual dream that remains vivid in memory, I find myself thinking it is high time to bring back the stocks and the whipping post. Likewise for stupid drunks, but I have already vented enough about Larry.

❧

True to his word, Desmond did call mid-morning from the university library where he was working. He told me that after leaving my apartment, he and Larry had returned to the hotel. While Desmond telephoned room service for something to eat, Larry raided the mini-bar where he managed to polish off the two small resident bottles of gin. Food arrived in due course, and half way through his club sandwich Larry passed out again. By this time Desmond had found his patience stretched so thin that he simply let Larry lie where he had fallen and ordered up a movie.

The following morning Larry awoke feeling like death warmed over, drank a couple of brandies from the mini-bar, and announced he was taking the next train back to Toronto. Desmond showered and dressed, then went down to the coffee shop for breakfast. When he returned to the room Larry had packed up and left. Fortunately for Desmond the room had been charged to Larry's credit card, one of several. (For Larry, money is not a problem.) Desmond now planned to spend the day at the library, after which he was booked for dinner with the Chair of the English Department. The following day he would spend at the library, before taking an afternoon train back to Toronto.

"I'm sorry my schedule is so tight, Geoffry. I had hoped we might at least have lunch. But considering how things have played out, I don't want to stay any longer than absolutely necessary."

"I quite understand. And no doubt you will be returning to Montreal in the future. Let's have lunch then. These days I have plenty of free time on my hands. I'll take you to the Lord Elgin Club."

"That would be delightful. I understand the dining room is first rate."

"Speaking of the Lord Elgin Club, Desmond, why don't you come to Montreal for my party. Even if you didn't know Elinor you'd be more than welcome. Perhaps you could rustle up a little academic business and write off the weekend on your income tax."

"What a good idea. I'll certainly see what I can do."

I asked Desmond for his address and telephone number, which I jotted down on my telephone pad. "Desmond, before I say *au revoir*, could I ask a favour, not too onerous I hope?"

"Of course."

"The Harold Baldwin of whom we spoke has a wife, an ex-wife it would appear. Do you think you could find out where she lives and let me know, along with a phone number, if she is in the book. I would like to speak with her, but at the moment my reasons are a bit unclear. I do not intend to make harassing calls, or pester her for money. When all is clear to me I will tell you the whole story. I know it is a strange request, but I would appreciate the information. She may be using her maiden name, which I do not know."

"Of course I'll see what I can find."

"If you are in the least bit uncomfortable about my request please say so. You hardly know me, after all."

Desmond laughed into the receiver. "I know you better than you may think. Larry has told me about you. Believe it or not, he holds you in very high esteem. I seriously doubt you will watch, beset, or harass Mrs. Baldwin, if that is indeed her name. Leave it with me. And now I must return to the salt mines."

"Stay in touch."

My plan, if such it could be called, was simplicity itself. Go to the source. If anyone could tell me the true story about Harold Baldwin it was his ex-wife and mother of my grand-children. That is, it goes without saying, if she would consent to meet with me. There was a bridge to be crossed, or burned, as the case may be. First I had to get in touch with my former daughter-in-law. An address and perhaps a telephone number would be a start.

∽

"Good afternoon, Ma'am. Am I speaking to Barbara Carstairs?"

"Yes, you are."

"My name is Geoffry Chadwick. I know that means nothing to you. Am I catching you at an inconvenient time?"

"No, you're not."

"Let me first assure you that I am not a telemarketer, nor a telephone salesman of any sort, I am not soliciting for charity, nor am I conducting a poll. I am calling from Montreal. My identity will surprise you. I have learned, only recently, that I am the natural father of your former husband, Harold Baldwin."

"Is this some kind of joke?"

"Indeed not. Harold was very recently in Montreal, and we met. In fact, as the result of an accident, he stayed with me for a few days. At first meeting the family resemblance was unmistakeable. I am astonished, as you probably are."

"If what you say is true, Mr. Chadwick, I am truly astonished. But why are you calling me?"

"I would like for us to meet, if possible. You are the mother of two children who are my grandchildren. One day I would like to meet them as well. Let me say right away that you do not have to tell the children who I am. I am not out to rock any boats or disrupt your life in any way. A divorce is disruptive enough without a second father-in-law coming out of the woodwork. I would like to talk to you about Harold. Who knows him better than you?"

The woman made a sound that could suggest either laughter or derision, perhaps both. "I thought I knew him when I married him. More fool I."

"Look, Mrs. Carstairs, I am seventy. My wife recently died.

I am not making a bid for sympathy, but you can understand that as a widower with no children I am naturally curious about my newly discovered son, not to mention my grand-children. Were I to come to Toronto would you be prepared to meet with me, say for lunch or dinner — at a restaurant of your choice?"

"I don't see why not. That's quite a long journey to make for just a lunch. But if you are willing to make the effort I will certainly meet with you, if only to hear your story. You said Harry had an accident. What happened?"

"A bicycle ran into him and broke his ankle. He stayed with me for a few days until he felt up to making the drive home. Didn't he tell you?"

"We don't speak very much. Hardly at all, in fact. And when we do it's strictly business When will you be coming to Toronto?"

"The sooner the better. How about tomorrow? I could take the early train and be there in time for lunch, a little on the late side."

"That would be fine. Why don't you call me when you have made your travel arrangements and we can decide where to meet."

"I'll do that. I very much appreciate your being prepared to meet with me. At first you must have thought me a crank caller."

Barbara Carstairs laughed into the receiver. "You're right. I was taken aback. But if what you say is true there has to be a good story that goes along with it. I'd be a fool not to meet you. Can I rest assured you are not going to stick a needle into my arm and sell me into white slavery?"

It was my turn to laugh. "Not only do I not have the inclination, I lack the imagination. Besides, who would look after the grandchildren? I'd have to hijack someone else to cook meals and do laundry. As I said, I do not wish to monkey with the status quo."

"Then I can breathe easy?"

"Very easy. I would ask one small favour. Would you mind not mentioning our meeting until after we have met and talked. I wouldn't want Harold to think I was sneaking behind his back, even though I am."

"As I said, Mr. Chadwick, Harry and I seldom speak. I didn't even know about his broken ankle."

"What can I say? By the way, as your once and past father-in-law I find Mr. Chadwick a bit too formal."

"What would you like to be called?"

"My name is Geoffry, with which I am comfortable. Please do not call me Father, Dad, Pops, Gramps, or any of those other diminutives which are acceptable in sitcoms but not in what passes for real life."

Laughter, warm and friendly, filled the receiver. "Geoffry it is then, and don't you dare call me Babs!"

"Point taken. I'll telephone when I have travel times."

᳘

My travel agent booked me onto the early morning train and reserved a room at the Sutton Place Hotel. It is quite possible to get to Toronto and back in a day, but to telescope that much travel into twelve hours means going by plane. I truly dislike flying. My aversion does not spring from fear. Should the plane decide to crash it's "So long, World," and no questions asked. A plane disaster neatly solves the troublesome problems of ageing: arthritis, bad backs, cardiac arrests, dental decay, fading eyesight, and the whole alphabetical list of debilitating ailments that accompany old age.

What I really dislike about flying is the infuriating way it depersonalizes the passenger. From the moment you step into the vast, bleak space of the terminal and join the line to check in, nudging your suitcase along with your foot, like an old, flatulent dog, you cease to be a person in three dimensions. The cast-iron smiles of the check-in clerks are balanced by the intractable scowls of security agents, who still manage to cop a feel with their metal detectors. I always try not to jump when the electronic wand whacks me in the nuts. To flinch suggests guilt, like heroin sewn into the lining or the jacket or marijuana tucked into the jockey shorts.

Then there are the hazards of other passengers: the man anxious to tell you how he put aluminum siding onto the garage with no help from the neighbours; the loquacious woman plying her needles en route to looking after her grandchildren while her daughter pops out another; the spotty adolescent wearing earplugs who has the volume of his IPOD cranked up so loud that the scatological rap song is clearly audible for three rows in both directions. I take no satisfaction from knowing he is damaging his hearing as my tax dollars will one day pay for his hearing aid.

The only way to fly is business class, possible only if the ticket is being paid for by the firm. Although I can readily afford to fly business class, my stingy streak forbids. Why pay megabucks for a slightly larger seat and a plastic plate of microwaved scrambled eggs. If I have to travel, I take the train. A wit once suggested that if God had intended us to fly he would have given us wings. This comic could not have been thinking of Canada, a country with too much geography and too few people. To get from Halifax to Vancouver by train is a retirement project, but Toronto remains a manageable distance.

The arrangements made, I went to my agent's office to pick up the ticket. Then, as the afternoon was only four hours old, I decided to drop in on Mother. As I was on foot I walked across the park. I am walking a lot these days, yet another, quite pragmatic reason I miss Elinor. She enjoyed driving; furthermore, she was a whiz behind the wheel. Elinor put paid to all those muscleheads who denigrate women drivers, the men with one hand on the cellphone and the other on their crotch, who steer with a hard-on. I can't remember the last time I took the wheel of our car, nor have I driven it since long before she died. I truly dislike driving, almost as much as I dislike flying. Between the bicycles, rollerbladers, geriatrics ignoring lights, jaywalkers, other drivers, cellphones, flatulent buses, roadwork, potholes, and traffic lights which have ceased to function, motoring just ain't the fun it used to be.

As I walked across the park, in the mellow, golden, autumn light, I wondered whether or not to tell Mother about Harold. The positive aspect was that it would give us something new to discuss. Conversational topics with a slightly loopy, moderately alcoholic woman in her nineties are circumscribed. Were it up to my demented sister Mildred I should most definitely not tell Mother lest it upset her. What Mildred fails to realize is that Mother suffers more from boredom than the usual ailments of the aged, hence the vodka; and that the most disturbing and disruptive presence in Mother's life is Mildred herself. Bursting unannounced into Mother's room and firing off volley after volley of caveats, injunctions, obiter dicta, and wrongheaded opinions, Mildred could give a three-toed sloth an anxiety attack.

Another reason for telling Mother is that were she ever to learn about Harold, she had better be told soon. She is an old lady who could die tomorrow, in a week, a month, a year. Having made it comfortably into her nineties, she is, as far as I am concerned, living on borrowed time. Who knows? Maybe the energizing news of a mystery grandson could jolt her into a few more years of sitting around doing nothing in particular. Since my recent life has been bound up in Elinor's illness, death, and funeral, I have little to tell Mother about the big world outside Maple Grove Manor.

The resident bore, a retired salesman, older than the universe, with badly fitting dentures, was hanging out as usual in the lobby, decorated in autumn tints. Old age protects him, sealing him off from censure like a patient in an antiseptic bubble.

By now he knows me by sight and wastes no time on the niceties of greeting. I do my best to head him off at the pass, but he has the true killer instinct of the old.

"These two old coons were making love," he began without preamble.

"Do you mean racoons, or — as the French call them — *ratons laveur?*" I crossed to the elevator, he following.

"No, no, I mean blacks, don't you know. Well, they were going at it hammer and tongs, when the old broad says, 'Careful, Honey, ah's got acute angina.'

"'Glad to hears it,' he says, ''cause your tits ain't that great!'"

He stood, wheezing with laughter as I stepped into the elevator and pressed the button to shut him out. One of these days a resident will run him over accidentally on purpose with a motorized wheel chair, and the world will be none the poorer.

Mother does not change. As a much younger woman she managed to appear insubstantial, as though a sudden loud noise or gust of air would cause her to disappear. She dressed in pastels, wore little makeup, spoke softly, and took up little room on the planet. As she aged she seemed to grow transparent. Colour leached from her hair, her skin, even her eyes. She gave the impression that light could pass right through her, that she cast no shadow, like the woman in the Strauss opera who can't have children but can still sing three long and demanding acts. All this was A-okay with me. Mother never got in my way, and I always managed to conceal my indiscretions. We never disagreed.

"Hi, Ma, what's cooking?" I kissed her pale, wrinkled, fragrant cheek. Twice a year I give her a bottle of Chanel No. 5, which she has adopted as her favourite scent. No Georgio or Rive Gauche for her, thank you very much.

"Oh, Geoffry, you're just in time for a little drink. Why don't you pour for two?"

Too late I realized I had forgotten to pick up ice. Warm vodka is not my cup of tea, to mix a metaphor; and if I went downstairs for ice I risked being ambushed by another bad joke. Drinks poured, I sat in the other "good" chair. I furnished the room with pieces from Mother's apartment in order to ease the transition, but as long as the television set works and there is a backup bottle of vodka in the closet she is perfectly happy.

"What's new, Mother? Any searing dramas running loose in the halls and bedrooms of Maple Grove?"

"Goodness me, no. Nothing ever happens here. We played Bingo yesterday. Tiresome game. I never win, perhaps because I can't be bothered to pay attention. Mrs. Grayson won the full card, or so she thought. Turns out she had claimed three spaces which had not been called. Can you imagine? When the error was drawn to her attention she was outraged. Threw her card on the floor and stormed out, rather difficult with a walker. Fortunately the full card was the final card, as she quite spoiled the mood. I shan't play again. Bingo is even more boring than crafts."

Silence followed, meaning the story had ended. Mother lacks a strong narrative sense; one has to surmise her train of thought has reached a conclusion.

"I have some news for you, Mother. Possibly surprising — at least it was for me."

"Really, dear." Mother paused for a swallow. "Do I have to guess, or will you be forthcoming?"

"To cut to the chase, Mother, I learned only recently, since my last visit here in fact, that I have a grown son I never knew existed."

"That's nice, dear. Will he take care of you in your old age?"

Mother's reactions to many situations defy prediction, so I continued gingerly.

"I don't think so. My old age is already upon me, at least as regards the old age pension. So far he hasn't bought me a house, or an annuity."

"Where does he come from? Or do I really want to know?"

"A youthful indiscretion. Let me spare you the details. It was so long ago, fifty years to be precise, that it's all a bit unclear."

Mother paused for two swallows, then held out her empty glass for a refill. I welcomed the interruption.

"I suppose all young men have to sow their wild oats," she said, reaching for the replenished drink, "but most of them don't end up with stray children wandering about."

"I'd hardly call him a stray, Mother. He has parents; his mother is still alive — and two children of his own. Your great-grand-children."

"Oh, dear, will I be expected to give them a cheque at Christmas?"

"No, I haven't met them yet. I'm not sure I will. It's all very new to me, my very own soap opera where I have been cast in a leading role. I have no idea how the story ends, but I will keep you abreast of any breaking developments."

Mother sat quiet, ruminating and drinking. "Will I get to meet him?"

"I don't know. He lives in Toronto. I want to size him up first, be sure I want to let him into my life, our lives. As I said, the situation is all so new and unfamiliar I don't know how it will play out. If the right situation presents itself, I will surely bring him by to meet you."

"I would like that, dear. Does he have a name?"

"Harold, Harold Baldwin. His mother's husband believed the boy to be his. As I said, it was a long time ago ..."

I was rescued, not by the bell but by a knock. A woman wearing a white lab coat entered. "Oh, good evening, Mr. Chadwick. I didn't know you were here."

"That's all right, Mrs. Coates, I was just leaving."

"Time to get in our wheelchair and go down for our dinner," said the woman briskly to Mother, busy draining her glass. I can only hope "we" are screwed securely into "our" coffin before the first person plural invades "our" life. Sweet Jesus, whatever happened to "you" and "your"?

Rhetorical question. Mother is being well cared for, and that for me is all important. Whether or not my genes will drag me into decrepitude remains to be seen. Maybe I'll send a bottle of good scotch to the Grim Reaper.

## 8

*T*he unfortunate aspect of travelling to Toronto by train is
that the most interesting part of the journey comes immediately upon departure. After pulling out of Central Station, the
train moves slowly through industrial areas where handsome,
art deco factories have been turned into upscale condos and
co-ops. Passengers look out at once working class stretches
of housing now undergoing gentrification. The train passes a
bluff dotted with high rises before pulling into Dorval Station.
One can watch planes taking off and landing while suburban
passengers scramble aboard and fill the empty seats. The most
interesting part of the trip comes when the train crosses one of
several rivers which give Montreal its claim to being an island.
The bridge is long, offering glimpses of several small islands, a
few with houses. Metaphor aside, crossing a bridge is always an
exhilarating experience, for me at least. The other side beckons

with promise and possibility, seldom fulfilled; but then I am far too old to feel cheated.

For a few heady moments after pulling out of Dorval I hoped I had been lucky; the empty seat beside mine had not been claimed. Nobody to crowd my elbows on the arm rest or breathe up my oxygen. Nobody to wait for that first, unguarded moment, when my attention flickers from the page, to launch an opening remark. "Is that a good book?" Nobody to open up a laptop computer and mutter darkly under his breath or to exclaim out loud, "Isn't that the limit!" and, deliberately or not, compel my attention. Most fellow travellers demand acknowledgment in one way or another; and the empty seat beside me came as a little gift from God, the Unitarian one, not the Muslim, Hindu, Hebrew, or Christian.

My triumph turned out to be short lived. The window seat across the aisle had been claimed by a no-longer-young man whose frosted hair and snug clothing could not disguise the fact he was never going to look thirty-five in the eye again. After peeling off his leather windbreaker and making rather an issue of folding it neatly to place on the seat beside him, he produced that most dreaded of objects, a cell phone. It is to be remembered that a welcome aboard message crackling through the antique intercom had specifically requested restricted use of cellphones while the train was in motion.

The passenger across the aisle had one of those resonant, slightly nasal voices that could peel wallpaper. After two calls of the "Well, she said to me ... And I'm like to her ..." variety I had him pegged as a telephone queen. Five calls later I upgraded him to telephone slut. My irritation growing with each call, I laid aside my magazine.

"If you are going to make more calls, would you be good enough to stand between the cars."

His reply was to give me what he considered a withering look and to punch in another number.

I continued. "Would you mind asking the other party to speak louder. If the entire carriage has to listen to this conversation we would prefer to hear both sides."

"You don't own this train."

"True enough." I pressed the button to summon the steward, at the moment collecting the complimentary coffee cups.

"Yes, sir?"

"The passenger across the aisle is annoying me with his cell phone."

The steward managed to look both stricken and craven; I could tell it was a pose readily assumed whenever a passenger made difficult demands. "I'm sorry, sir, there is little I can do."

"Then do that little! And remember: I'm a much better tipper than he will ever be."

Wilting under my glare, the steward held a whispered consultation with the cps (cell phone slut). Giving me a wan smile as he picked up my empty cup, along with the cookies wrapped in plastic film for chewing safety, he retreated down the aisle to the galley. The cps gave me another killer look and punched in a new number. As luck would have it, the train manager was lurching down the aisle. I made a peremptory gesture to snag his obviously unwilling attention. Reminding him of his welcome aboard message, I informed him that the cellphone across the aisle was seriously compromising my enjoyment of Via Rail's vaunted service. I was beginning to feel like someone in church, asking saints to intercede on my behalf. The manager's body language suggested I should disappear in a puff of smoke, but I was firm. After giving me one of those shit-eating half smirks, he held another whispered consultation with the offending passenger. No sooner had he left the carriage than the CPS launched into another call.

Laying aside my copy of *The New Yorker*, I stood, as if going to the toilet. As soon as the bleached blond had ceased to look at me and returned to his "She said/ I said" call, I reached out quickly and snatched the phone from his astonished hand. Dropping it onto the floor of the aisle, I stamped on it sharply, three times, until certain it would no longer function. At which point I picked up the damaged appliance and handed it back to the outraged owner, while passengers in the adjacent seats applauded. He jumped up.

"Why — why, you stupid old fart! I ought to slap you bowlegged."

"When a man your age strikes a man my age, in front of a car full of witnesses, the hills are alive with the sound of lawsuits." I reached into a side pocket for my card case and extracted a business card, which I handed to him. "Send me the bill for a new phone."

Uncertain of how to react, with many pairs of eyes watching, the CPS snatched the card, tore it into four pieces, and tossed them onto the floor. "Just because you have one doesn't mean you have to act like one!" he declaimed as he flung himself back into his seat.

That was a pretty good line, and I was sorely tested not to laugh out loud. Instead I sat and took refuge in my magazine, while the train trip continued in blessed quiet.

After a couple of Bloody Marys, lunch on a tray, and a snooze with the seat tilted back, I watched the train pull into Guildwood Station. The CPS, who had been sitting, apparently lost in thought (unfamiliar territory I should imagine), exploded to his feet, made an issue of resuming his windbreaker, and flounced down the aisle. The leather shoulder bag he carried, not to mention the stylish suitcase he yanked from the rack, suggested money was not a problem. Dignity was, and I could see him taking off down the platform without having tipped the steward. I'd be willing to bet he was a man who would keep the baby and the bathwater, only to throw out the bath.

As the train began to move at reduced speed towards Union Station, I was obliged to reflect on my mission, for want of a better word. I intended to sit down with a woman I did not know and ask pointed questions about a man I had only just met. I am not given to quoting the Good Book, cause of so much mayhem in the world; but lines from *Ecclesiastes* came to mind: "In much wisdom is much grief: and he that increaseth knowledge increaseth sorrow."

Harold Baldwin had come into my life at a time when I faced a huge emotional void. Kinship aside, I had liked him at once, finding him bright and congenial. How disappointing it was to learn he might be considerably less endearing than I had initially believed. How I would have preferred not to hear what Desmond had so casually disclosed. How I could have wished he had paid me the simple courtesy of not smoking in bed and singeing the pillow. But the damage had been done; the genie was out of the bottle, and his unfortunate presence had obliged me to board this train and endure that silly bitch with the cell phone. To be sure, while I was seething inwardly over his banal, intrusive calls, I had not been brooding over Elinor or Harold. Elinor would have applauded my objecting to the nuisance; she would not have endorsed my stamping on the phone. Unfortunately Elinor was no longer around to keep me in check, and how I wish she were.

The train slid into the darkness of Union Station and came to a gentle halt.

Taking a taxi straight to my hotel, I left my bag and walked two blocks to the restaurant where I was to meet Barbara Carstairs for lunch. Since I was coming all the way from Montreal for the meeting, she had agreed to drive in from Markham. The restaurant we had decided upon turned out to be generic Italian, with pottery much in evidence and blue checked tablecloths that matched the curtains. The room also had a row of booths, more conducive to conversation than a random table; but it was to a table I was led by a hostess, whose slow, seductive smile could not conceal the fact that her blond tresses showed a good half inch of dark roots.

Although I arrived at the restaurant a good twenty minutes after the agreed upon time, Barbara Carstairs had not yet put in an appearance. She had, however, made a reservation. I requested a booth. Her smile glued firmly in place, the hostess tossed her mane, the colour of ripe corn, and led me to the side wall. After requesting a vodka and clamato juice I sat, facing the door, so as to be more readily visible. My soul longed for a dry martini, gin, straight up, twist; but prudence dictated something less lethal. Furthermore, the desultory array of bottles over the bar, festooned with plastic grapes, suggested the house gin might well have been distilled in somebody's washtub.

A woman entered the restaurant, looked around, spotted me, and walked directly to the booth.

"You have to be Mr. Chadwick," she said, extending her hand to shake.

"I was when I got up this morning. Please sit. Will you have a drink?"

"What a good idea. Gin and tonic, please."

I gave the order, then turned my attention back to my former daughter-in-law. Barbara Carstairs had the look of a woman for whom every waking minute must count as two. Her "toilette," as once was said, leaned towards the minimal. Shoulder length auburn hair, whose copper highlights looked natural, had been pulled back sharply from her face and fastened with elastic. Lipstick on a generous mouth turned out to be her only cosmetic, but wide cheekbones and impeccable skin would have made making-up a waste of time and concealed her natural radiance. Her look was either L.L. Bean or Land's End: navy blue turtlenecked pullover, denim skirt, gym shoes, admittedly comfortable for walking on city pavement. What looked like a pebble on a thong around her neck and gold stud earrings completed the outfit, along with a Swatch on whose failing battery she blamed her late arrival.

Her absence of anything remotely resembling chic must have grated on Harold. Most gay men want their women flamboyant: big hair, oversized jewellery, makeup applied as if for the stage. Barbara's total absence of artifice only threw into relief a genuine beauty. Her smile lit up the room and when we shook hands her grip was firm. I should imagine she was the kind of nurse whose mere presence in a room would cheer the patient. I liked her at once.

"How was your trip?" she inquired.

"Routine. There was a small incident with a cell phone, but it passed."

She smiled. "You were right when you said the family resemblance was strong. I think if I saw you passing in the street I would suspect you were related to Harry."

I signalled the waiter to bring me another drink, the first having gone down fast.

"Seeing as how his name has come into the conversation, I am anxious to learn more about this newly discovered relative."

"What precisely do you want to know?"

"Anything and everything." Briefly I sketched in how Harold had called "out of the blue," as Mother would have said, and suggested a meeting, I told of our first encounter, the accident with the bicycle, and the visit to the hospital, followed by his staying with me for a few days before being driven back to Toronto. I also gave her a heavily edited version of what Harold had already told me about their marriage, so as to avoid covering the same ground twice. Finally, I told her about Desmond's observations, unexpected and unsettling, concerning both his family and his job. "So you see, Barbara, I am frankly perplexed about this new and unexpected presence in my life."

We ordered, and Barbara began to talk, hesitantly at first; but, spurred on by a second gin and tonic, gradually with more candour. Over a routine Italian meal, helped along by a respectable bottle of chianti, Barbara told of her life with Harold Baldwin. I suspected she too was applying a mental blue pencil to some of the less seemly episodes, partly to spare my feelings and partly from a natural reluctance to reveal too much on first meeting with a total stranger, regardless of relationship.

What emerged was the portrait of a man who would never be caught putting a milk carton into the blue box reserved for recycled newspapers. His motto, had there been a family coat of arms, could well have been: "A place for everything and everything in its place." For a woman dealing daily with the disorder of illness and death, the lapse of putting a marmalade jar onto the top shelf of the refrigerator instead of into a rack on the inside of the door seemed minor. Not so to Harold. As a working mother, Barbara admitted to not keeping a spotless house; only the foolhardy would eat off her kitchen floor. Two small children only added to a general confusion to which Harold could not or would not adapt.

The peace of early marriage turned into an armed truce with the birth of children; a girl, followed two years later by a boy. Harold liked the idea of children, but not the children themselves, irrational creatures who made unreasonable demands on his time. They made noise, did not hang up their clothes, wanted their artwork taped to the refrigerator door, and generally impinged. Harold did not take kindly to fatherhood; the armed truce escalated into open hostility. At first, aggression limited itself to words, barbed comments on Barbara's many inadequacies, as a cook, housekeeper, parent. On one occasion she retorted that if he would only dirty his hands and his soul and work in the marketplace instead of isolating himself in an academic, poorly paid bubble, then she could take time off from the hospital and turn into the *Good Housekeeping* wife he appeared to want. Until that time he might think of shutting up. That was the first time he slapped her. Too astonished to react, she stood rubbing her burning cheek as he slammed out of the room.

He apologized and bought her a blender. Barbara laughed and said she would have preferred a fur jacket or a gold bracelet, but never look a gift blender in the blades. One night he lost his temper with the children, who had pinched the batteries from the TV remote for some purpose of their own. They did not seem suitably contrite, at least to Harold; and he began knocking them around. Barbara stepped in to stop him, and he slapped her again. This time she did react and slapped him back. Enraged, he began to beat her about the head and shoulders with closed fists. Screaming, the children rushed to her defense, punching and kicking their father. Realizing he had crossed into an emotional No-Man's-Land, he left the house and stayed away for five days.

When he returned, as though nothing had happened, life continued. New batteries were bought for the TV remote; the marmalade jar found its random way into the refrigerator; Barbara urged the children to hang up their outdoor clothing. But the marriage had ended. The night of his return Harold slept in the guest bedroom, from which he never returned to the conjugal bed.

Barbara knew he was having problems at work; but communication between them had dried up to discussing household maintenance, children's schooling, and — inevitably — money, always in short supply. Barbara came to realize the children would be better off alone with her than in the toxic atmosphere of a ruined marriage; it was she who filed for divorce.

As she told me about being chronically hard up, I remembered Harold telling me he had private means, an annuity I think he said. Yet I remember Elinor complaining more than once about the cost of raising children, not to mention grandchildren. What with school fees, clothing quickly outgrown, unexpected illness, bags of food consumed, and the childhood faith in the bounty of Santa Claus, the communal bank account saw many lean years. I had no experience with the cost of raising a family, so I could only hope Harold's money went toward household maintenance and raising the children.

Or was I simply equivocating. Uneasy, I changed the subject.

"Was he having an affair?"

"I don't know. I am inclined to think not; but if he was, he covered his tracks. No lipstick stains on his shirt collar, stray matchbooks in jacket pockets, long blond hairs snagged in the tweed jacket. As you can see I love old movies. If he was having a *cinq-à-sept* it must have been between twelve and two, as he always came home on time, if only to shut himself away in his study with his books and computer and cigarettes."

"Was he always a heavy smoker?"

"Very. Most of the time he was careful about ash trays, but even the most careful smoker has accidents. He used to smoke in bed; I hated it, but I was still being the good little wife. One night he fell asleep, and his cigarette burned a large hole in the new duvet he bought me for Christmas." Barbara laughed. "I would have preferred diamond earrings or a designer handbag. However the burn in his brand new duvet bought, you may be sure, for himself, made him angry enough to quit smoking in bed. I did not want him blowing smoke around the children; on that I was firm, so he used to smoke only in his study. The children were never to go into his room without permission, but the odour was strong enough to keep anyone out. As a trade-off I agreed not to leave hair in the sink or lipstick on the towels. I suppose you could call it a compromise, more of a standoff really."

I gave a shrug. "Is he giving you some financial help, at least with the children?"

"He gives me an allowance, enough to send the children to private schools. He quit his job, as no doubt you already know; and when his father died Harry expected a pretty fair legacy. However, what he finally ended up with turned out to be a lot less than he had expected. Consequently, I have to keep on working."

"I see." The standard conversational filler was not accurate. I did not see. How, with supposedly a sizeable inheritance from his putative father, could Harold be cutting corners with his own family. Either he really was strapped for cash, or he was concealing the true amount of his income and paying less child support than he could afford. The idea that he might be cheese-paring with his own children disturbed me. I had a daughter from my first marriage, but she died in the same accident that killed her mother. Up to only recently I had not been aware of my grown son. But I had been raised to believe in accepting responsibility for one's life. My father believed in responsibility more strongly than he believed in God, and scorned those who manipulated piety in order to avoid paying their dues. Like my father, I believe that if you bring life into the world you thereby incur an obligation. The idea that Harold might be short-changing his own children made me a little bit crazy. For better or for worse they were my grandchildren.

On the point of asking about these same children, I observed Barbara staring at my watch, a basic Rolex Oyster that does not rely on dying batteries to tell the time.

"Goodness me, it's after three; and I go on duty at four. I'm afraid I'll have to dash. I tried to find someone to cover for me, but we're very short staffed at the moment. I hate to eat and run, but I must."

"May I call you?"

"By all means. Do you want to meet the children?"

"Yes, but not right away. I am still getting my head around the idea of a son. There will be time for grandchildren when I get things sorted out. Now, off you go. I'll settle the cheque and walk back to the hotel."

We shook hands across the table, and Barbara hurried off, leaving me with a welter of impressions that I would have to consider and classify. If my suspicions turned out to be correct, Harold had been economical with the truth. Worse still, he may well have tailored the truth to suit his purpose, whatever it was.

I can easily imagine that for a fastidious man, not to mention a gay one, life with a woman like Barbara must have its lumps. Good-hearted and candid though she may be, living with her must mean overlooking or denying oneself many of the small graces that ease the transition through a day. A little dust on surfaces does not bother me, but mold in the shower does. Windows do not have to gleam, but drinking glasses must.

Long hairs in the sink or blocking the drain in the tub erase the memory of these same tresses spread out on a passionate pillow. The ebb and flow of the moon must disappear from the conjugal bathroom before the morning shave.

Perplexed, uneasy, and just a little bit drunk, I walked back to my hotel, checked into my room, and lay down for a nap. It was after eight when I awoke, too late to make any plans for the evening. I could have called Larry, but I did not much want to see him. Ditto for my sister Mildred, who would scold me for not giving her advance warning I was to be in Toronto. I did not feel hungry enough for another restaurant meal, nor did I want to scramble off to the theatre or a concert. Instead, I ordered up a club sandwich from room service and a movie. I also took a shower. I was paying for this room, so why not enjoy it. And in my present frame of mind I was far better off alone.

# 9

Hardly had I let myself into my apartment and put down my overnight bag than the telephone began to ring. Having just endured the boring return trip from Toronto, mercifully without cell phones, I decided to let the answering machine take the message. Oftener than not callers hang up without speaking, mute testimony to the transient unimportance of most calls.

After unpacking and taking a quick, restorative shower, I sat at my desk to deal with two day's mail. The message light on my telephone blinked insistently; and I punched in my date of birth, the code one is routinely advised against using, to retrieve messages about which I was quite incurious. There were several messages, the first being from Dwayne Durnford virtually shrieking into the receiver his regrets about being unable to attend the party. Another queen who can't dress,

Dwayne confuses flamboyance with style. Who today still wears bell bottoms. He is now too old to kiss and tell, so he just tells. Several hostesses have learned to their dismay that he bites the hand that feeds. If you invite him to a party he will say it was tacky; don't invite him and he will say much worse. He did, however, come to the funeral service. As a matter of fact I am sorry he won't be there, as he does help to make a party go. And his outfits are always good for a snide snicker.

To my surprise my sister's voice, resonant and intrusive, came on to announce that she had tried repeatedly to reach me and that I must be away or not answering my telephone. In any case I was to call her as it was imperative that we speak. What Mildred considers important does not necessarily coincide with my hierarchy of values. Considering that we were raised in the same household by the same parents, together we could knock the nature versus nurture theory out of the loop. Mildred lives in a world of inflexible values and received ideas: the tensile bond between family members, the joys of a Christmas party, the importance of showing up at funerals, the indisputable cuteness of their pets, the need for magenta impatiens in a shade garden, and the importance of returning telephone calls at once, if not sooner.

Were I to telephone now I would not be interrupted while I was watching the news or eating my sparse meal. Tapping out Mildred's number, I braced myself for the onslaught. Mildred only calls when something is on what passes for her mind, so I mentally circled my wagons.

"Geoffry! I've been calling and calling. Have you been away? Or were you just not returning my calls?"

How like Mildred to put me immediately on the defensive. Not about to admit I had been to Toronto without telephoning her, I muttered something about a friend from out of town who had been monopolizing my time.

"What is on your mind, sister mine? We spoke only recently, when you were in town for the funeral."

"I called Mother. My goodness, Geoffry, she is becoming so forgetful. It worries me dreadfully. I just don't know what we are going to do."

"We are going to do nothing. Mother is comfortably into her nineties. She is being well looked after. She makes no waves. The staff at Maple Grove all love her. Why tamper with success?"

"I suppose." There followed a pause; I knew the real reason for the call was now due. "Geoffry, I telephoned Mother because I thought I had left my gloves in her room, the ones I wore to the funeral; and she told me you have a son."

"So it would appear. He certainly looks like me. Whether or not he has inherited my sterling qualities remains to be seen."

"But, Geoffry, people just don't have grown children walking into their lives. Mother tells me you had no idea. Are you quite certain?"

"No, Mildred, I have known all along I had a son in Markham. It was my guilty secret. I have been living a lie, scarcely able to face the world. And so forth, and so on." I paused to draw a deep breath. "Of course I didn't know. His mother, whom I diddled fifty years ago during a college dance, didn't tell a soul until only recently. Her husband, now dead, thought the boy his. Apparently she has become quite dotty with age and blurted out the truth to the boy, now a middle aged man, only recently."

"But are you going to acknowledge him, as your son I mean?"

"I don't see why not. Anybody seeing us in the street would know we were father and son. Would you have me slam the door in his face?"

"Of course not!" Mildred sounded more indignant than usual. "But you know what they say. 'The sins of the fathers …'"

"'… are visited weekends on the sons.' I can't be very enlightening, Mildred. The situation is completely new and unfamiliar. To say I'm playing it by ear is the understatement of the year."

"Naturally." Another pause followed. "But, Geoffry, now that this — this man — Mother tells me his name is Harold — has come into your life, will it affect the way you think about — about your future?"

The light bulb flashed on over my head. "Do you mean am I going to put him into my will?"

"Well, since you put it that way."

"Yes, I do put it that way. You have been melting down my telephone to learn whether or not I intend to disinherit my nephew and nieces in favour of a man I have known less than a week. Mildred, you truly are something else. Instead of rejoicing that perhaps I may have a new interest, a son to keep me company while I grieve for Elinor, a companion for my old age, all you can think about is whether or not I am going to cut your brats out of the will — or substantially reduce their inheritance."

"Now, Geoffry, don't get upset."

"I am upset. I fucking well am upset. (Mildred usually chides me for profanity, but now she wouldn't dare.) Luckily for you your children are Father's grandchildren. It is for his sake and not yours that I will not shortchange his legitimate heirs. Much as you may regret the fact, I am not dead yet. And with Mother's genes I may be around for a while. Who knows. The bottom may fall out of the market, or I could develop an expensive habit for designer drugs, or fall under the spell of some teen-aged temptress who will take me for everything I've got. There's many a slip 'twixt the cup and the lid of the coffin. So for the moment you can put what you presume to call your mind at rest. I have not called the notary; nor do I intend to.

"Now, if you have one silly millimeter of the instinct for self-preservation you will hang up. To quote the Bard: 'Stand not upon the order of your going, but go at once!' The next sound you hear will be a dial tone. Good night!"

I hung up, well and truly steamed. What is it about members of the family and their ability to get under your skin? Yet why did I allow myself to get all worked up? Mildred was born a silly cow, and age has only made her more so. Besides, there is nothing like a shit fit to get the adrenalin pumping. As a matter of fact I felt pretty good at the moment. A drink was most definitely in order. And even if Elinor were here to point out that I had been unduly hard on my sister, I would have borrowed a line from the silver screen. "Frankly, my dear, I don't give a damn!"

౨

When I included R.S.V.P. Regrets on my invitations I meant precisely that. Telephone to say you can't come to the party; full stop. A number of people, whom I hope will spend eternity locked into a phone booth in Hell, called to say how delighted they were to be invited and what a wonderful idea it was to have a party instead of a memorial service and how much Elinor would have loved the idea and what a shame it was she couldn't attend her own party. I tried to be polite and express delight at their being able to attend, all the time wishing they would get the hell off the line and get themselves a life.

About to pack it in and let the answering service take messages for the rest of the evening, I saw the next call was long distance, the 416 area code. As I did not recognize the number as being that of my sister or Larry, I decided to risk a reply. My initial "Hello" must have sounded defensive, as laughter came down the line.

"Geoffry? It's Desmond, Desmond Langley. I was in Montreal recently with Larry. Relax. I am not trying to sell you anything, nor am I soliciting for charity."

From sheer relief I too burst out laughing. "Desmond! What a surprise. I've just been fielding calls from people calling to tell me they are coming to the party — in open defiance of my R.S.V.P. Regrets. Either they can't read, or they flunked sandbox. What can I do for you?"

"Dinner, the dinner we failed to accomplish on my last visit. It turns out I need a couple more days' research at the McGill Library, so I'm coming down to Montreal for a long weekend. Two questions: One, will you have dinner with me? Two, can you recommend a reasonable hotel that is not a flea bag? I'm travelling on my own credit card this time, and frugality is the password."

"Answer number one: I'd be delighted to have dinner. Answer number two: Why don't you use my spare room? It's sitting there vacant; and since you're going to be at the library all day you'll hardly be underfoot, waiting to be diverted."

"That's very kind, Geoffry. Please, please don't think I was hustling an invitation."

"I don't. And even if you were, what's the harm? Why pay rent for a room you will hardly use? I can cope with breakfast. One night we will eat out. For the other evenings you may have plans; otherwise we will send out for barbequed chicken, pizza, Chinese, whatever. You will not be overwhelmed by gracious living."

"Sounds far too good to refuse."

"I'll most likely be here when you arrive. If not, I'll leave a key with the doorman."

Desmond laughed. "I promise not to steal the spoons."

I found myself laughing at the idea. "It's all right if you do. I'm insured."

After settling details of time and date, we said *au revoir*. For the first time in a long time I hung up the receiver in a positive frame of mind. I had liked Desmond, and the prospect of having him to stay for a couple of days pleased me. Now was just about the time Elinor and I would have poured ourselves a "little drinkie," so I poured my second drink of the evening. The first had been a result of my sister's phone call. As I resigned myself to a solitary evening of television, I realised Desmond's presence would keep solitude at bay for a couple of days. And, thank goodness, we were in no way related. There had been no mention of Larry, but I felt certain his name would come up in due course.

For the next day or so, I was preoccupied with turning over Elinor's house to Jane. This transaction involved a visit to the notary at which Jane wished me to be present. I had no real contribution to make, other than keeping the seat of a chair warm; but, ever punctilious, Jane wanted everything to be up-front and centre. She understood her brother and his wife were to have first choice of the contents, other than the family jewellery that went directly to Jane. Such jewellery as Elinor owned, aside from a heavy gold chain and some gold bracelets, ran to large, semi-precious stones, with great presence and moderate value on the insurance policy. These pieces would quite overwhelm Jane, whose taste in gauds ran to lockets and cameos; but perhaps her daughters would one day grow into them.

Jane may have a tight sphincter, but she is not a fool. She realized how easy I had made it for her to take possession of

Elinor's house and portfolio, transactions over which I could easily have dragged my feet; as a result, she appeared to have overlooked the contretemps arising from the funeral, and was as pleasant as I could remember. She declined my offer of lunch, pleading the need to collect the children from here and there. We parted with a promise on my part to come to dinner as soon as Jane and her family had settled into the new house, an evening I did not anticipate, but one I felt obliged to undergo. Elinor would have expected no less. It went without saying that both Elinor's children had been invited to the party, and both intended to be present.

We left the notary's office with Jane in full possession of her mother's house. The status quo bothered me less than I had feared. It was, after all, only a house, and without Elinor's animating presence no more than a piece of real estate similar to many in the community. I was glad the place was now Jane's responsibility, and I walked away with a feeling of relief that the deed had been done.

Plus there was the weekend with Desmond as my guest to anticipate. I almost laughed. Had I come to the point where I measured out my life in coffee spoons? As a student, all those decades ago, I swam against the current and disliked T.S. Eliot at once. When the explanatory notes to a poem are almost as long as the poem itself it's time to head back to the drawing board. It goes without saying I was a majority of one; to my classmates, Eliot wrote sacred texts. The *Gita*, *Koran*, *Bible* all paled beside *The Waste Land* and *Four Quartets*. Does anyone outside of graduate school read Eliot today? Rhetorical question. I have never seen anyone on the subway reading *The Collected Works*, but I seldom take the subway, so the random sampling is flawed.

౿

Desmond arrived in the mid-afternoon, a problematic hour I have always thought. It was too late to offer him lunch and too soon to begin drinking. We compromised on tea and a ginger snap at the kitchen table.

"I had lunch on the train," he explained. "Helps to pass the time. I could have taken a plane, but by the time you get out to the airport, go through security, and board, the trip takes almost as long as that by rail. Besides, I feel safer on a train. If only they could make planes the same way they make the black box, I'd be glad to fly. Should there be a mishap, the black box always seems to survive, which is more than you can say for the plane."

"I hadn't thought of it that way," I said. "What I dislike about flying is the way the experience manages to erase all individuality. I feel like a thing in an airport, not a person. Maybe it's all part of a vast conspiracy to persuade us to stay home, an option I find more to my liking with each passing year."

I put down my mug; cups and saucers are just to pissy for my present way of life. "What's the news of Larry?"

Desmond shrugged. "I could ask you the same question. I seem to have fallen from grace since that unfortunate weekend.

I telephoned a couple of times, if only to thank him for picking up the hotel tab; but he was either not at home or not answering. Finally I left a message on his voicemail, but the call was not returned."

"In spite of Larry's being one my oldest friends, I am going to be disloyal and suggest you're probably better off. Larry requires enormous amounts of care and feeding. To have him as a friend is far more than a retirement project; it's a career. In my book the only people who can get away with that kind of behaviour are those who have exceptional talent, or beauty, or personality — some compensating quality that makes putting up with them almost worth the effort. But Larry? What does he have to offer aside from dated gay chatter, wide open legs, and an astonishing capacity for gin."

Desmond smiled. "I suppose you're right, and you have certainly known him a lot longer than I; but I think fundamentally he's a kind man."

"So are we all, when it suits us. Most of us would pull little old ladies out of snowbanks, avoid treading on children, and rescue a kitten from a rain barrel. Nothing more than any properly raised person would do. But when kindness collides with self-interest, when doing the right or ethical thing involves self-denial — 'Ay, there's the rub.' And I wouldn't count on Larry unless the sky were blue, the grass green, and the little birds sang, 'tweet, tweet, tweet.'"

Desmond laughed out loud. "Mr. Chadwick, you take no prisoners."

"Not any more. Certainly not since Elinor died. And a big, messy, lemon meringue pie right in the kisser for those airheads who tell me not to be bitter and resentful, all garnished with sickening platitudes about death being a part of life, no more suffering, and God's will. I am bitter and resentful. And — on the off-chance that there is a God, which I seriously doubt — He, She, or It — is either colossally stupid, or inept, or else a real prick. Any nitwit with two years of high school could do a better job of running Planet Earth than the absentee landlord to whom people pray on Sunday."

Desmond tried hard not to smile. "I was reading *Mary Poppins* the other day."

Suddenly we were both laughing at full volume. I held up my hands, palms outward.

"Enough. I did not invite you here so I could vent. It's just that my fuse is shorter since Elinor died. And — just to wrap up the Larry question — I no longer have room in my life for someone whose idea of a good time is to drink until he is well and truly soused."

Desmond nodded. "Neither have I. On that we both agree."

"Perhaps you'd like to unpack and take a shower. I always feel gritty after a trip."

"Do I have to?"

"No."

I could see Desmond attempting to stifle laughter. "Good. I'd really like a shower, but I thought it might be a house rule. I don't want to blot my copybook."

"Geoffry, She-Wolf of the S.S., gives you permission to withdraw."

Desmond reached up and tugged his forelock, then backed out of the kitchen, bowing. I was secretly delighted. It takes brains and imagination to be seriously foolish. I already knew Desmond had brains; I was glad to encounter the imagination.

∽

By the time Desmond had showered, it was time for a drink. I was relieved to see he had pulled on a sweater over his button-down shirt, meaning I did not feel obliged to put on a tie. Decades of being what the young today call a "suit" has left me with a profound disinclination to wear a tie unless the occasion cries out for one. I wore a tie to Elinor's funeral. I put on one for the aborted dinner with Desmond and Larry. I will buy a new one for the party, no more than a pro forma gesture as all my ties are the same: medium width, conservative stripes or repeated small objects — anchors, spurs, flags — but no polka dots. Around such key decisions, to wear or not to wear a tie, does my life now pivot. A hypothetical observer could well tell me to "get a life"; but I had a life, a good life. I don't have it any more, and I am too old to tackle the Grand Design with a view to changing it for the better. Trivia will do just fine.

"This is very kind of you, Geoffry, letting me stay."

"The favour is mutual. Having a warm body in the place, especially one who can string three sentences together and come up with an idea, is a genuine pleasure. You know, before I married

Elinor I never minded being alone. Solitude never seemed the less favourable choice. Now, however, I am relearning how to live with myself. The blandishments of youth no longer beckon, and with retirement I find there are a great many hours in a day."

"Believe it or not," began Desmond, setting down his glass and resting suede elbow patches on corduroy knees, "I understand perfectly. I don't know whether Larry told you, probably not; but I was married, for almost twenty years to be precise. I have two children, of whom I am distantly fond. When my wife divorced me because, if you can believe, she fell in love for a second time with her high school sweetheart, I was secretly and shamefully delighted. By then I had realized my real orientation was not as a skirt-chaser; and much as I genuinely loved Laura, I was glad to be free. She took the children, with my blessing, and has done a splendid job of raising them to be reasonable human beings."

Desmond paused for a thoughtful sip of his whiskey. "But much as I enjoyed being free to go out — I'm sure you can join the dots — I came to realize there was much about the relationship I missed. Laura and I had our routines, habits, ways. Our — conjugal life — had dwindled to near zero, but we were hugely compatible. We actually talked to one another. Then she met an old beau who got the juices flowing. I know the symptoms because I was experiencing them with a teaching assistant. Am I boring you?"

"Not in the least. I listen and learn."

"There's not much more to the story. We divorced, amicably. There was no drama, no wrangling over settlements, no 'I gave you the best years of my life and you are not taking the paintings!' But suddenly I found myself living alone and not liking it very much. I was well past the age for all-night sessions of drink, drugs, and sex. Just try teaching the freshman survey course with a bad hangover. True, I was having a sex life, of sorts; but, corny and naive as it may sound, I wanted a love life. Love is more than tumescence. I wanted more from a relationship than dinner, followed by sex, followed by nothing. You know the old gag: You too can have the body of a twenty-one year old — but you have to buy him a lot of drinks first."

"Enjoy a passionate sex life. Get cable."

We both laughed. My own laughter sprang from two sources: first, the corny jokes, and second, the sheer pleasure in wanting to laugh.

"Could I have another of these?" asked Desmond

"Of course. I'll join you."

Drinks poured, Desmond resumed his ruminations. "I realize that I am certainly not alone in hoping to find the ideal partner, one of those Platonic ideals promoted tirelessly by movies, TV, and a surprising number of novels. Larry was just one more in a series of might-have-beens; he seemed so sane and sensible when we met, at a wine and cheese rout. It's difficult to get roaring drunk on wine, and it wasn't until I first saw him dive into the martinis that I came to realize he did not arrive without baggage. And even without trying to match him drink for drink, a course of action that would have sent me into detox, I still drank more in his company than I usually do. There I was, once again teaching the freshman survey course with a hang-over. Definitely not the way to go."

Desmond leaned back in his chair. "But enough about me. Where would you like to have dinner? You know the city better than I."

"How about Italian, not too high end, within strolling distance?"

"Sounds good."

"I'll call and make a reservation."

Over uneventful, unthreatening, unsurprising pasta and veal, Desmond and I drank chianti and talked.

"I appear to have been monopolizing the conversation," he said. "I'm a bit hyped up just being in Montreal; and," he smiled at me across the table, "to your misfortune you are a good listener."

"I only listen when I want to. You know something, Desmond. I guess by now you have figured out I have lived on both sides of the fence; but I am more comfortable around men who do not look on women as the enemy. Far too many gay men treat women as a foreign species, not completely hostile, but not trustworthy either. Larry is a prime example. The only women he consorts with are clients and fag-hags, or fruit flies, or whatever the currently hip term. Most such women I have known in the past require huge amounts of attention. Their acceptance comes at a price; among other demands they require long hours on the telephone, and they have to be told every fifteen minutes that they are looking wonderful. I find them exhausting."

I paused to pour more wine, the waiter having disappeared. "There is something I would like to discuss with you. Do you remember, during our evening with Larry, that I asked you about a certain Harold Baldwin?"

"Yes, I do. I'm afraid I didn't find much good to say about him."

"I know. And although I tried not to let on, I was quite taken aback. You see, I recently had a telephone call from said Harold Baldwin ..."

Between bites of veal I told Desmond of Harold's coming to see me, our relationship, his accident, his enforced visit, and the blossoming friendship. I related how I had gone overnight to Toronto to meet his divorced wife and how her albeit edited version of events only served to reinforce the negative side of Harold's personality.

"So, Desmond, you can see that I am frankly perplexed. Here I sit at almost seventy, a grown son wanting to be part of my life, and burdened with the knowledge that he may be a bit of a shit."

Desmond put down his knife and fork. "I'm sorry, Geoffry. Had I known he was your son I would have minded my remarks."

"Don't apologize. Please! I wanted your spontaneous reaction. Had you known the situation I might never have learned the truth. He certainly was plausible and charming in his dealings with me. I suppose I am just thinking out loud, using you as sounding board."

"I'm glad you did. It's quite a tale. Now, may I make a suggestion?"

"By all means."

"Let me begin by saying I don't want to sound like a self-help manual, *Parenting for Dummies*, or *12 Steps To Being A Better Father*. But play the situation by ear. You have no real commitment to this man. It was by merest chance you learned of him in the first place. It's not as though you have to pay his way through college, or set him up in business, or buy him a car. He made himself known to you, well and good. He took the initiative. Let him prove that he merits being called your son, in the complete sense of the word. If it turns out you grow to like and admire him, good. If not, are you any worse off than before he telephoned?"

I smiled. "The voice of reason. I guess it comes from being a university professor. Aren't they supposed to be much smarter than civilians? As a matter of fact, you have suggested the very course of action I had pretty well intended to follow. But it is reassuring to have my point of view reinforced by someone who has two brains to rub together."

Desmond inclined his head. "Thank you, Kind Sir."

"More wine?"

"Half a glass. I don't want to be hungover tomorrow; it's going to be a long day. If you manage to snag the waiter's attention ask him to bring the check."

It took us a while to pay up and get out. The worst of the summer tourist season was over, but the restaurant was still more crowded than usual. I suppose I should applaud the influx of visitors and their contribution to local coffers. The annoying feature is that the season is open only for tourists and not on them, meaning it is forbidden to shoot strangers, even when seated at one's favourite table. I suppose this represents progress, but I still have doubts.

～

I lay in bed, pillow under my knees to ease my back, but sleep refused to come. It often does these days, but tonight my mind raced in overdrive more than usual. To begin with, just down the hall in my guest room lay a man I would very much like to have sex with. Furthermore, I had picked up encouraging vibes. Desmond would not openly state he was both ready and willing, the result of a natural tact that was one of the many features that made him attractive to me. But when you have bumped around the circuit as long as I have, you learn to decode the subliminal signs: the lingering glance, the ready laughter, the body language suggesting intimacy rather than distance. That is why gay men are better at what used to be called seduction than straights. It has been said that women need a reason to make love; men only need a place. When your garden variety slob is having an attack of must, all his other senses appear to shut down; and he comes on like a randy elephant. Elinor used to say that God gave men a brain and a penis, but not enough blood to run both at the same time. How else can one explain rape and prostitution? Just imagine having sex with someone who isn't the least bit interested in you as a person. The mind shuts down.

To be sure, sex is not an equal opportunity situation. There are losers in love: the hugely overweight, the deformed, the dimwitted. I know it is very sad, but there you are. I happen to have been one of the fortunate ones which, I suppose, is another way of saying I never lacked for people to have sex with. And now that "Eighty is the new seventy," it would appear I have been given a reprieve. I am frequently told that I do not look my age. Those making the observation are being kind; to insist on the appearance of youth is a socially acceptable form of stroking. The ineluctable fact remains that I do look my age, but I have not yet openly started to decay. I still have my hair and my vision; I have not put on copious amounts of weight; and I do not begin stories with the phrase "When I was a boy."

Yet here I lay, alone, when only a few steps away slept a man, handsome, trim, intelligent, and — according to Larry, who ought to know — well endowed. I had not lost my interest in sex, especially with the right person; and Desmond qualified on all counts. It has been a long time since I felt that particular electric charge, yet I had chosen not to follow through Why?

Alone in the dark, I checked off my reasons. Aside from the transient pleasure of sex, I could see no future for Desmond and me, even if we did manage to hit it off. A tenured professor was not about to pull up stakes and relocate in Montreal, and I am far too old and settled to contemplate moving to Toronto.

Unlike many Montrealers I happen to like that city very much; but spending an agreeable few days is one thing, creating a whole new life another. So even if Desmond and I were to embark on what once was called an affair, it must remain just that, a relationship based on infrequent meetings, telephone calls, occasional joint vacations, and the inevitable entropy that must of necessity follow enforced periods of separation.

Another considerable drawback was the difference in our ages, a good fifteen years. With each successive birthday the gap would widen. By the time Desmond turned seventy, I would be eighty-five, the old eighty-five. That is provided I had not been called to Abraham's bosom. Had I been forty-five and he thirty we might have swung it. But he must one day wake up to the realization that his lover is an old man. Better to have Desmond as a friend.

My final and most pervasive reason for not pursuing involvement with Desmond was the absent presence of Elinor. She would have been the last person in the world to expect, or even want, a post-mortem constancy. Yet I, a homosexual man who had lived through the tentative Fifties, the promiscuous Sixties, the worldly Seventies, the terrifying Eighties, and the rapacious Nineties, was prepared to remain faithful to the memory of a dead woman. It sounded like something from the worst kind of sentimental Victorian gothic, and perhaps it was. Yet even gothic scenarios, with all their mise-en-scène of moonlit ruins, shadowy staircases, creaking casements, made allowances for a reappearance of the dead, often translucent and wearing a long, diaphanous mumu. I could almost envy those who believe in an afterlife and their comforting hope that one day they will be reunited with their beloved dead. I held out no hope of seeing Elinor again, either here or there. Were I to subscribe to this harmless fantasy, how could I expect to find her, whole and vigorous as when I first knew her, or wasted and withdrawn with illness.

I grieved because I could not hope to see Elinor, or my father, or any of a score of people who have touched and changed my life. It was a bleak and cheerless prospect, but happy thoughts could not uproot the yews to replace with apple trees in bloom. I must also remain vigilant lest grief degenerate into self-pity, an indulgence of which I deeply disapprove. So did Elinor.

Some decisions resist rigorous analysis and reject the $A+B=C$ formulae of analytical thought. What is intuition but a short-circuit of the logical process. However I had arrived at my decision did not matter. What counted was the goal. Elinor had been my last love, and such she would remain.

At the same time it was oddly reassuring to realize I had passed the age for flings. I was through looking at ceilings. I no longer kneel, even in church. No more stuffing pillows under asses, or soaping up someone in the shower, or scrubbing grass stains off my knees. Sixty-nine was merely the number between sixty-eight and seventy, my present age. It was time to turn in the sweater with the big scarlet A for available. I liked Desmond; I really liked him. I found him sexy and bright and attractive. And I still knew it was better to have him as a friend.

I must have fallen asleep. I did not wake up, as I usually do, for an early morning pee. By the time I shuffled out to make coffee, Desmond had left. A note on the counter told me he would telephone later in the day.

As I drank the coffee he had made and read the morning papers, I realized how pleasant it was to be alone, freed from the obligation to make nice in the morning. I guess I had crossed a kind of emotional Rubicon. But as I sat quietly, reading the op-ed page and sipping my coffee, I had to admit the opposite bank was not an unpleasant place to be.

The glances over cocktails
That seemed so sweet
Are less enticing
Over shredded wheat.

# 10

*D*esmond turned out to be the ideal house guest, almost too ideal as I scarcely saw him for the rest of the visit. Having arrived on a Thursday afternoon, he spent Friday in the library, then went out to dinner with a few colleagues. He invited me to join them, but I begged off. The evening's talk would revolve around academic and scholarly topics, from which I would be excluded; and I did not feel like making the effort to meet new people. I knew Desmond's invitation was *pro forma*, a courteous gesture; and when I fudged he did not press the issue. It must have been a convivial evening, as I had already gone to bed when he got home.

The following morning I managed scrambled eggs and muffins before Desmond headed off once again to the library. We said goodbye as he left, as he planned to go straight from the library to the station for a late afternoon train to Toronto.

"This really was very kind of you, Geoffry," he said as we shook hands. "I'd like to come back when I have a bit more time. We could visit some galleries, have a long lunch, maybe go to a movie."

"I'd like that very much," I said, meaning it. "The spare room is here, seldom occupied. Just let me know when you'd like to use it."

"Well, off I go. 'Once more into the stacks, dear friends.'"

The day being fine, I decided to walk over to Maple Grove and look in on Mother. She prefers me to visit in the afternoon so that we can share a drink or two, but with or without my presence she will knock back a few before supper. In a curious kind of way her pre-prandial drinks insulate her from the petty feuds and internecine struggles endemic to residences filled with the old and the idle. By the time Mother is wheeled down to the dining room, she is a bit glazed and answers all questions and directives with a vague smile and a faraway look which might suggest she is considering the subject at hand. However, she resists information the way a teflon pan resists butter; it sits on the surface but fails to penetrate. As a result even the most disagreeable and dogmatic residents have given up trying to enlist Mother to their pet peeves and causes. The staff love her. She creates no fuss and is unfailingly pleasant. She says "Thank you" for services rendered and tips generously at Christmas. As a result she is well looked after, and that for me is the so-called bottom line.

"Why, Geoffry," Mother tucked the lapels of her robe closer

around her neck in a reflex gesture of modesty. "I didn't expect to see you in the morning. Shouldn't you be at the office?"

"I'm retired, Mother. I have been for almost five years now."

Sensing rebuke, Mother wilted.

"Sometimes I forget myself that I no longer have to go to the office," I fibbed. "Just the other morning I was stepping into the shower when I remembered I had nowhere to go."

Mollified, Mother leaned forward. "I had a call from your sister this morning. I was surprised. She seldom telephones in the morning, just as you seldom visit before lunch. But, my word, she was quite worked up. It appears she tracked down your son, Harold Baldwin, in the telephone book and invited him for dinner."

"She did what!" I snapped, unable to keep the edge out of my voice.

Mother bristled slightly. "I said she invited your son for dinner. He has broken his ankle, but he manages quite handily with a cane."

When characters in novels grow really angry they are said to see red. I did not see red so much as a pair of hands, not unlike mine, around a throat, not unlike my sister's. Unsure of what to say, I said nothing. On a roll, Mother needed no further encouragement.

"Mildred thought it might be nice for her children, all of whom happen to be in Toronto at the moment, to meet their new cousin. Just imagine, after all these years, her grown-up children are meeting their grown-up cousin for the first time.

I find it all quite exciting. Don't you, Geoffry?"

"I'm jumping right out of my skin, Mother."

How like that interfering bitch of a sister to move right in and preempt Harold as if he were her own. Mildred is a widow with a comfortable income and not enough to do. I have long suspected her husband died just to get away from her. She is forever telephoning City Hall to complain of an old mattress left in a lane, or an overflowing litter basket in a nearby park. She telephones the CBC to remonstrate over points of grammar, more precisely usage, about which she considers herself the ultimate arbiter. She e-mails PBS to complain about the number of begging letters she receives in the mail. Couldn't the money be better spent on programs. She chides panhandlers, even as she drops a two dollar coin into the upturned hat. She scolds strangers for littering and snaps at dog owners who fail to scoop. She is a king-sized, grade-A, ne-plus-ultra pain in the ass. I have no doubt she blurted out any amount of background information on the family, tales which had no business being told to strangers.

I suppose I am partially to blame. Having told Mother about the newly discovered Harold, I should have realized she would pass the story on to my sister. Starved as they are for topics of conversation they must have fallen greedily on the idea of a brand new grandson-slash-nephew. Can you imagine? Who would have thought? Isn't Geoffry the limit. You're never too old to be surprised. I simply can't wait to meet him.

In spite of the old saw, it is not idle hands that make mischief but idle tongues. What perplexed and annoyed me is that I would never know exactly what Mildred had volunteered about the family to her new nephew. She shoots from the lip, and when she is excited about something she tends to lose the sense of discretion that filters out information best left under wraps. We are not a family with shameful secrets, but I do not want Mildred, or anyone else for that matter, offering a crash course on Geoffry Chadwick. I can't honestly call Mildred a liar, but she has a way of distorting the truth that can be almost as misleading as falsifying it. If she wants to deal in misinformation it is a free country, just so long as the bent truths are not about me.

Unwilling to pursue the subject of Mildred and Harold lest Mother see how pissed off I really was, I suggested there was a news story I wanted to catch on Newsworld. I turned on the television set and we watched in silence for a few minutes, long enough so that Mother would not think I was cutting my visit short. Lunch at Maple Grove is served on the dot of noon. I made good my escape and walked back to my apartment to simmer down.

Mildred has three grown children, two daughters and a son. I still tend to think of them as children, although they are all in their thirties; and Richard, the eldest, must be uncomfortably close to forty. Tall, blond, and handsome, he is a fussy fairy, with the habitual expression of someone who has a piece of gone-by fish or overripe cheese under his nose. Nothing is ever quite right for poor Richard. Shirts come back from the laundry missing buttons; neighbours have boisterous children and noisy pets; steaks ordered rare are routinely overcooked; bugs dine out on the plants in his windowboxes; and the postman routinely ignores the No Flyers sticker on his mailbox. Like fish in water or birds in air, Richard lives in a constant state of pique.

When I first learned he was gay, some years ago, I thought I might find him a kindred spirit. My wish was not to be cosy and intimate, giggling over our small debaucheries like girls at summer camp. I have always disliked that particular brand of gay freemasonry but I did hope that Richard and I might be able to communicate in the kind of shorthand that presupposes a certain point of view, without all the dots having to be joined. It turned out we had nothing to communicate. Never have two gay men had so little in common.

Richard is a musician. No harm in that. I am very tolerant of musicians. Some of my best fucks are musicians. My nephew, however, played the organ and the harpsichord, furthermore in public. Many years ago I told him he would never get a job playing honkytonk harpsichord in a whorehouse. Without a glimmer of humour he told me he wouldn't want one. Like most young musicians he imagined himself as a world renowned performer, but the bleak reality proved to be otherwise. People do not camp out on the street in order to have first choice of tickets for harpsichord recitals, not to mention that the advent of talking pictures put many an organist out of business. Nothing if not enterprising, Richard has carved out a niche for himself in Toronto. He is organist and choir director at one of the major churches, St. Something-or-Other, with a large budget for music and a small one for dogma. He teaches the harpsichord to private pupils and gives the occasional recital. It was just such a concert that prevented him from attending Elinor's funeral. To be fair, he was prepared to cancel and reschedule; but I persuaded him the show must go on.

Elizabeth, the middle child, is now married and living in Calgary. I convinced her that flying east for the funeral would have been a waste of time and money. Instead, I invited her to the party, and so far she has not telephoned regrets.

Like her brother, Elizabeth started out to be a musician, in her case a singer. She came to Montreal to study; and after her prim and conventional upbringing in Toronto, the gallic *joie-de-vivre* of the French city hit her like a powerful drug. In short order she had made quite a name for herself, but not as a singer. In fact, she was spending so much time on her back I feared she might develop bunions on her ass. The voice was good, a strong lyric soprano that might have developed into a true spinto. But she lacked the burning drive for a performing career.

Instead, she married a man who had built up a successful trucking business from before scratch. He began as a long-distance driver and ended up as president of the company. To borrow an expression of Mother's, he is "a diamond in the rough." Immensely likeable, he nonetheless exudes an aura of menace; to cross him would be unwise. Whether or not he was aware of my niece's colourful past, he obviously made it perfectly clear that he would tolerate no nonsense. In short order they had five children, and Elizabeth changed from being a freewheeling, live-for-the-moment broad into a den mother and pillar of the community. Her children are bright, handsome, and polite. She also holds down a job as church soloist. Her life appears to suit her, and I am glad. Four or five times a year we have a long talk on the phone.

Jennifer is the youngest daughter and the pick of the litter. She has none of her brother's prissiness or her sister's slapdash approach to living. Her brunette beauty only improves with age. How a pain in the wazoo like Mildred could have produced such a delightful daughter is one of those mysteries perhaps best left unexplored. Once she was engaged to an eligible and personable young man, who had only one drawback: he was gay. Fortunately she found out before the ceremony and escaped with no more than bruised vanity, not a terminal condition. Then she met a peppy young lawyer who, unlike her former fiancé, did not "respect" her. In fact, he showed so little respect that their first child was born six months after the wedding. They now have two more children, and the marriage shows every sign of surviving, no mean accomplishment. I consider Jennifer more than a niece; she is a friend, and I hope she will come to the party. A sick child prevented her from attending the funeral, but she wrote me a charming and touching letter. With Jennifer I feel I exist for her even when I am not in the room.

I decided to give her a call. With small children constantly underfoot, no time is a good time to telephone, so I took a chance.

"Jennifer?"

"Uncle Geoffry! What's up?"

"Is this an inconvenient time to talk?"

"Couldn't be better. It's a beautiful afternoon, and the children are outside with the neighbour's kids laying waste to the garden. I've decided to give up on grass and go for astroturf. How are you doing?"

"As well as can be expected, whatever that means. To be perfectly candid, I have seldom felt more bloody-minded, although my health continues good. I'm doing my best to plug the hole in my life, with little success; but I soldier on. However, I did not telephone in order to vent but to ask you a question. You recently met my newly discovered son. What was your take on him?"

"Am I about to enter a minefield?"

"Only if you fail to tell me the truth. Seriously, Jennifer, the fact that this adult Caucasian male happens to be my son, the result of a youthful indiscretion, does not mean he is clad in white samite."

"White what?"

"Samite. It's a kind of fancy fabric, sort of a track suit for saints."

"Right. You most remember, Uncle mine, that I spend a good deal of time in the company of children. They chatter nonstop, but vocabulary is limited; and the subject of samite hasn't yet come up."

"Point taken. But I repeat: what is your opinion of Harold?"

"Before I answer, let me give you a bit of context. Richard and I were summoned by Mother to meet our new cousin; one might have thought we were to have an audience with the Pope or tea with the Queen. You could have tripped over the protocol; it was to be strictly family — no husbands, partners, or significant others. Brad fed the kids and got them off to bed while I dug out a dress and the ironing board. Six-thirty on the dot."

"I take it Mildred was a little revved up."

"On amphetamines. The table was set for best; china, silver, crystal. To be fair, she can't use her good stuff with the kids, so most of the time it's melamine, and stainless cutlery, and plastic tumblers. But she really laid it on: avocado stuffed with crab, boeuf en daube ... Hang on a minute, Uncle Geoffry; the kids are playing what looks like Spanish Inquisition. I'd better check it out."

Over the line I heard Jennifer's raised voice issuing a series of unilateral directives, followed by injunctions, followed by threats of recent baking to be withheld. Then she returned to the phone.

"Sorry about that. But an ounce of prevention. Anyway, the guest of honour arrived half an hour late but armed with roses and apologies. It's been a while since anyone gave Mother flowers, and she was immediately won over. She even allowed him to smoke, even though she frowns on cigarettes."

"*Et alors?*"

"What can I tell you. He certainly looks like you. Heavier, and the hair is dark. But otherwise he's a clone. The resemblance ends there. You are a loveable old bastard; he is too smooth by half. Charm by the yard. With two kids of his own, I doubt he is gay; but he flirted with everyone, including Richard."

"A simple question. Did you like him?"

"Yes and no. How can one not like someone who is knocking himself out to be agreeable. On the other hand, I couldn't help thinking he may have an agenda. I don't know what, and maybe it's petty of me to be suspicious. But I couldn't shake the feeling I was watching a performance. Curtain up on a drawing room set. Agitated family. Enter from stage left the rediscovered relative, in a white samite dinner jacket."

I laughed into the receiver. "You sure know how to hurt a guy. Was the evening bearable?"

"Up to a point. Mother got onto her high horse and told family stories. Richard and I have heard them a hundred times, but she too was on a roll and out to charm. Between Harold and Mother it was almost like a contest, last round of the charm-off finals. Even sourball Richard was nonplussed. But I have to admit the man is bright and funny and attractive. Those Chadwick genes ..."

"Flattery will get you everywhere."

"Uncle Geoffry, I think I'd better go. The Goths appear to be sacking Rome over what remains of my rose bushes. I'll call tomorrow when the offspring are heavily sedated."

"Off you go — to save the eternal city."

After hanging up the phone I sat for a moment. Jennifer is solidly grounded; her shit detector finely tuned. Her appraisal of Harold did not surprise; nor did it reassure. As for my sister, I could just hear her blurting out tales of the family, most of them harmless, but some better left unrelated. Mildred likes to give the impression that she comes from wealth. Granted, she has never gone hungry or ragged; but she is anchored in a time when being a millionaire meant holding colossal wealth. Today's billionaire is yesterday's millionaire; but Mildred, like Hyacinth Bucket, likes to lay it on thick. I know for a fact she shops at Wal-Mart and Costco, and wouldn't enter a quality store except during the post-Christmas sale. She is a foolish female; but she did produce Jennifer, and for that I must cut her some slack.

Later that night, as I awoke from the edgy unconsciousness that these days passes for sleep, I replayed my conversation with Jennifer. As I did so, I began to realize that my niece, at less than half my age, demonstrated far more acceptance of my son than I, his biological father. To be sure, she had been spared some of the unsavoury details that I had come to learn. Still, I wondered if perhaps I had been guilty of the same short-coming I have often deplored among those friends who are parents, namely a wish to overlook faults in their children and to present them to the world as paragons. I suppose it is natural for parents to airbrush their offspring into near perfection and in so doing to underline their success as parents. My son the doctor has a more pleasing ring than my son the bank-robber.

Why should I have expected Harold to enter my life trailing clouds of glory. Why expend the effort to be upset because he turned out to be a fallible human being instead of a walking compendium of those North American virtues I had been raised to admire. Unlike other parents I could not indulge myself in pleasurable hand wringing while I wondered where did I fail as a parent. I had absolutely nothing to do with the way he turned out, so why not simply applaud the good and ignore, or at least accept, the bad. After all, I had not even put him up for adoption, so I could not luxuriate in that particular guilt trip, should I be so inclined. (I wonder if those enterprising, adopted children who track down their birth parents sometimes regret finding the sorry specimens who brought them into the world. But that's another avenue of speculation.)

Nor could I smugly admit to a distaste for making value judgements, with my own values as the gold standard. I make judgements all the time, about behaviour, dress, politics, food, decorating schemes, and jogging shoes worn downtown. What is more pleasurable than sitting in silent judgement on a person, only to find he (or she. "Rest In Peace Political Correctness," as Elinor used to say.) does not measure up. How deeply pleasurable it is to decide that the hapless individual standing in the dock of disapproval is not as intelligent, witty, charming, erudite, or amusing as advertised. What greater joy than to dismiss his intelligence as second rate, his wit as derivative, his charm as specious, his learning as superficial, and his humour as juvenile. We all do it, I more than Elinor, although even she enjoyed delivering the occasional put-down. I doubt I could have lived with her otherwise.

There remained the thorny problem of the burned pillow. We were no longer dealing with differences in taste or values but the deliberate ignoring of a request. I might almost say a parental request, if only it didn't sound so pompous. Besides, he was a bit old for a clip on the ear or having his allowance withheld. Supposing I could banish him to his room, he would still smoke away the time out. Of course, there was nothing in the fine print stating I was obliged to house him whenever he came to Montreal. Let him incinerate someone else's bedding.

I knew I was being petty. One cigarette burn in a pillow can hardly be called a major dysfunction in the cosmic scheme. But goddammit! — that burn really pissed me off.

Brooding about this silly situation was not about to send me back to sleep. I rose and prowled into the alcove off the living room where I keep the TV. I flicked it on and dial spun at random, settling at last on what appeared to be a porno flick. I guess the station assumed that by three a.m. the tiny tots were in bed. A caucasian woman was being quite graphically screwed by a black man. Both had good bodies plus the necessary equipment. What on paper must have sounded like a real erotic scenario turned out to pack all the sexual punch of line dancing. To begin with, her hair, neatly rolled around her head, must have been lacquered into place as her sexual gyrations failed to dislodge a single strand. She was naked except for large button earrings, and shoes, not just any old shoes but circa 1935 evening shoes, with high heels, pointed toes, and a T-strap around the ankle. Were I to have been in her place I would first have removed the earrings, then the shoes, followed by the rest. The man also wore two items of clothing: a kind of shorty bathrobe and a condom, visually even more of a turnoff than in practice. All this activity was taking place in what could have been a greenhouse filled with tropical plants, most of which looked carnivorous. I suppose safe-sex porno is to be applauded in the age of rampant STDs, but I still couldn't get past the shoes.

I flicked off the set and returned to bed quite cheered up. If that film was what passed for erotica in today's scene I was glad to have turned in my testosterone.

჻

Having just poured my first cup of coffee and unfolded the morning papers, I heard the telephone give its unwelcome ring. The display panel indicated long distance with a 416 area code. It being well after six a.m., the regular rates were now in effect; however, now that most people have some sort of telephone contract the old rules no longer apply. Elinor used to refer to daytime charges as mink rates, as opposed to the after six p.m. muskrat rates. The telephone continued to jangle. I took a tentative sip of coffee and answered.

"Chadwick?"

"Larry, what's up?"

"I was afraid if you recognized my number on the display screen you wouldn't answer."

"It is a bit early in the day for a social call."

"I wanted to catch you before you went out." A pause followed. "I was naughty when I was last in town, wasn't I."

"Yes, you were."

"I'm sorry I fucked up the evening. Believe it or not, it won't happen again."

"Believe it or not, Larry, I've heard those words before."

"This time they have the ring of truth. I have no other choice."

"How so?"

"In a word, since I was in Montreal I have had some heavy sessions with my doctor. Just before I saw you last I had a whole battery of tests, asshole to elbow. When I went to see the shaman about the results he was not a happy camper. I won't bore with sordid details, but it looks as though I am on the wagon for the rest of my life."

"That's a sobering thought. Sorry, I don't mean to be flip."

"I'm not a well woman — and my liver is like cottage cheese. If I continue to drink I will die. Nobody likes the sauce more than I — as well you know — but not enough to croak for."

"I'm glad you feel that way about it."

Larry laughed. "It's not much of a choice really. Live or die. I'm like Susan Hayward: 'I want to live.'"

"Do you have an immediate plan of action?"

"Indeed I do. Everything I have heard and read suggests that when you make a major change in behaviour you have to rethink your whole life. I'm closing the office and heading off to Europe, just as soon as I possibly can. To get away from Toronto for a while will help the transition to sobriety."

"Good idea. Where will you go?"

"I don't know yet. Someplace where a long cocktail hour is not part of the culture. Italy for a while. I shall drink gallons of San Pellegrino and eat quantities of pasta."

"Don't substitute food for sex. People who do end up not getting into their own pants."

Larry laughed again. "It's so long since I had sex when I was sober I've forgotten what it's like. One day at a time, as the saying goes. But I'm getting out of town as soon as I possibly can, which means I won't be coming to the party for Elinor."

"Far better you get away. A party where guests will be drinking heavily is no place for you at this point. The best way to avoid temptation is to avoid it. How long will you be away?"

"I don't know yet. Until I get sick of the vagabond existence or I feel I can cope with life in Toronto sans gin — a terrifying prospect I have to admit."

"Is it chiseled in stone that you have to live in Toronto for ever and ever, amen? There are other cities, and once you are fully retired you may well want to live somewhere with a more congenial climate."

"I hate to admit it, Chadwick, but you're right. I haven't really thought that far ahead. I'll have more perspective when

I'm beaded-bagging it down the Via Veneto. Anyway, things are going to be pretty hectic for the next few days, so I may not get to call again before I head out."

"Not to worry. Send me a card when you have an address, and I'll respond in kind."

"Well, well, I guess that's about it. The final chapter is about to begin. Bummer, but there you are."

"As my old granny used to say: 'Don't grumble; don't crumble.' And don't be a stranger. I'm only a postage stamp away."

"What the hell! They say change is inevitable — except from vending machines. I may even call, at some ungodly hour when you are fast asleep."

"These days I'm never fast asleep. Call whenever you like. And have as good a trip as possible, under the circs."

"As they say in your benighted province: 'I'll do my possible!' More anon."

By now my coffee was cool enough to drink, but I ignored the paper spread out on the dining room table. To my surprise I found myself "of two minds," a foolish expression from my youth. Not surprisingly, I was pleased to learn Larry planned to get his drinking under control by taking the most radical step, namely to stop cold turkey. If he really stuck to his proposed regime we could meet as just plain folks and not as adversaries. Instead of relegating Larry to the fringes of my life, I could welcome him back in as the good friend he once was. Were he not to drink, then neither would I. *Quid pro quo.*

And yet, I had to admit that once again I was being jostled into an awareness of "time's wingèd chariot." That Larry, the most hyperkinetic man I have ever known, had been faced with the ultimate black-white choice only served to remind me that time was indeed running out. Almost to my surprise I found I did not much mind. To borrow Larry's expression, my final chapter began the day Elinor died. Whether Harold Baldwin would turn out to be an episode or merely a footnote remained to be seen. In the meantime, I believed Larry had made the right decision: to radically change his life and to blast himself out of the familiar rut. Was there a trip in my future? Perhaps, but not until after the party.

Well, well, well, good on Larry.

I poured another cup of coffee and returned to the paper.

～

After my shower and shave, I was seized with an irritated restlessness. My daily agenda being clear, I decided on impulse to visit my fitness centre, a.k.a. gym, for a workout. Since the funeral, and before, I have not been going to Fitness Over Forty, a registered trademark. I heartily dislike exercise unless there is some useful end, like gleaming windows or a well-shovelled walk. But to lift weights and lower them, to walk and go nowhere, to row and remain forever in the same place reminds me of the punishments visited on mythological figures in pre-Christian Hell: to fill a bottomless well with a broken pitcher or to roll a stone endlessly uphill.

For a while I had what is laughingly called a personal trainer, to be sure, some people get quite personal with their trainers, and their after-hours exercise sessions provide fodder for gossip columns. In my case, I could not have felt more impersonal about my trainer. He came heartily recommended by an acquaintance of Elinor's, and I agreed to undertake a series of six trial sessions. A musclebound, unshaven lout, he had decided to become a personal trainer rather than attend university; at least that was his story for the press. My suspicion is that any institution of higher learning that requires the ability to read and write would have turned him down flat.

I explained, or attempted to, my limitations of age and arthritis, not to mention moderate anxiety and creeping anomie. He appeared to listen, and we went to work: chest curls, lateral extensions, squats, manoeuvers with a large, inflated ball that bordered on the indecent, and exertions on machines that looked as if they might be used by Torquemada on Niccolò Machiavelli. In between these bouts of extreme effort I stretched, leaning into a corner with my palms flat on the wall, grasping my hands together behind my back than raising them, and pulling my knee towards my chest. (For part of this humiliating experience I had to lie on the floor, a position that erodes dignity.)

On occasion I emboldened myself to ask, "Are you sure this is good for an arthritic joint?"

"Just the ticket. Got to get the old joints turning over. Think of exercise as oil."

Was he not the expert? Was I not paying him in coin of the realm to guide me safely through this unpleasant experience? Who was I, in my sedentary sixties, to question this paragon of fitness? The answers came the following morning when I had difficulty getting out of bed. At first Elinor thought I was performing a kind of Saturday Night Live sketch, but a barely controlled snarl convinced her otherwise. I ached in muscles that for over sixty years I did not know I possessed.

In short, I had to postpone the next two sessions. The trainer and I had a little talk. When I explained I did not aspire to the Olympic Games he seemed puzzled. By then I had figured out for myself which exercises I should avoid. The remaining sessions were mostly a waste of time. He stood around glumly while I said yes, I will do this; no, I won't attempt that. By the end of the sessions I had cobbled together a basic program which I could execute on my own. For a few weeks I worked out doggedly, three times every seven days.

The annoying feature was that I could determine no real benefit as a reward for the effort involved. I had not lost weight, not that I needed to. I felt no more flexible; the same joints still ached. The bathroom mirror sternly told of gravity overcoming good intentions. I could not fake a greater sense of wellbeing. When asked, "Does working out make you feel better?" I wanted to answer, "Better than what?"

Then Elinor became sick, and the urge for regular exercise went on hold.

But perhaps the time had come to resume my workouts, if

only to give a focus to three mornings of each week. I might even shop around for a trainer in his or her forties, someone old enough to realize weight bearing joints are not forever.

Having been away from the gym for some weeks, I started off slow, not vigorously enough to work up a real sweat. I dislike showering with strange men, almost as much as I abhor male changing rooms, mute testimony to the universal truth that nudity is a luxury few of us can afford. Luckily for me late morning is a slow time; I was the only man working out, so I was mercifully spared testosterone talk with paunchy men attempting modesty with a tiny towel.

Back in my apartment I did a little mental bookkeeping and decided my workout had earned me a Bloody Mary, more precisely a shot of vodka with just enough clamato juice to buy off the Fates. It was delicious, and moreish. After a second pop I ate some cheese and tottered down the hall for one of the best naps I have enjoyed in weeks.

So refreshed and revitalized did I feel that I decided to walk over to Maple Grove Manor and look in on Mother. I love the golden late afternoon light of autumn. Halloween was only days away. As a child I loved the last night of October, ringing doorbells and getting something for nothing. I think I would almost gag today over the junk candy my friends and I eagerly carried home in baskets and pillow cases. A few reckless people gave out money; it is to be remembered that I speak of the time before UNICEF boxes were virtuously proffered. A few cheapskates handed us apples; it was, after all, the harvest season. These bulky objects took up unnecessary room in our baskets; furthermore, they were heavy. Our solution was to line them up on the streetcar tracks and watch the number 14 tram car turn them into applesauce. (Almost as much fun as putting a penny on the train tracks, but that's another story.)

The streetcars are long gone, along with the childhood friends and the wish to eat sweets. That particular urge disappeared once I began to drink, and scotch is a lot easier on the teeth.

A few of the Maple Grove residents sat in lawn chairs outside the front door, bathed in the last rays of sun. They nodded and said good afternoon after the manner of the old, eager for a little contact, however glancing. Once through the door, I was ambushed by the resident bore.

"Hey, Geoffry, did you hear the one about the blonde who went to see her doctor who told her she was pregnant?"

"Yes, Sir," I replied.

Only momentarily put off by my counter-attack, he pushed ruthlessly on. "She asked the doctor, 'Are you sure it's mine?'"

As he gasped and wheezed, as always his own best audience, I escaped up the stairs without waiting for the elevator.

Mother was comfortably into her first drink of the day. The attendant nurse had coaxed her into some clothes, a long, wraparound skirt and an evening sweater aglow with gold braid and shiny beads. The garment quite overwhelmed Mother, but then almost anything does.

"What's up, Sparkle Plenty?"

"Well, Geoffry, I've only just hung up the telephone after

talking to your sister. She had so much news I could barely take it all in. She had her nephew, your — son, to dinner and to meet the family. Apparently he is perfectly charming, and the spitting image of you. Of course, you do take after your father more than me. Poor Craig. If only he had known. But Mildred said the man couldn't possibly be an impostor; she just knew the second he walked through the door that he was your son."

By now I had poured myself a weak drink as prop to keep Mother company. She was on a roll, so all that was required of me was to sit still and listen.

"They spent a delightful evening. Mildred was sorry when he had to leave, but it appears he has a cast on his foot and it is very tiring. Richard drove him home."

Mother paused to drain her glass and I took the cue, filling the tumbler with much water, little vodka.

"Thank you, Dear. The best part of all is that Mildred is going to drive him down to Montreal to meet me. Won't that be exciting? Just fancy; I will meet a grandson I never even knew I had."

Slightly flushed with excitement and vodka, Mother showed signs of the prettiness she once had. Like pentimento, the traces of her former beauty were faint; but she had managed to captivate Father, and he had been a truly handsome man. His photograph stood on her dresser in a silver frame badly in need of polish. It showed a middle aged man who faced the camera squarely, smooth hair, square jaw, candid gaze, someone who had lived comfortably in his skin.

"Where will Mildred and Harold be staying?" I asked with slight alarm, remembering the cigarette burn in my pillow.

"They will most likely stay with a friend of Mildred's — I can't remember her name. But you will come over, won't you, Geoffry. Just imagine; Craig's son and grandson right here in my room."

"Don't forget Richard. He qualifies on both counts."

"Yes, of course, Dear, but we all know about Richard."

"Is Harold going to jump out of a cake?"

"Out of what, Dear?"

"Oh, nothing, Mother. Certainly I shall come over. Did Mildred say when they would be coming down?"

"She wasn't precise. Harold's cast will be coming off shortly, and he would prefer to wait until then."

"Makes sense."

Mother took a hefty swallow. "What a pity Elinor won't be here to meet him."

For once I agreed wholeheartedly with Mother, although I could imagine Elinor's reaction of laughter and teasing. Were I writing a self-help manual I could do a nice riff on an unexpected new life turning up to replace one lost, and the cycle continues. I could, but the scales did not hang in balance. I would trade fifty Harolds for one Elinor; However, the choice was not mine to make.

In the meantime I could not help realizing how this unexpected discovery of a grandson had energized Mother and given a focus to her life. Once she had managed to wrap her slender

intellect around the notion of my having a son, she had discovered a brand new interest to stimulate her circumscribed
existence. A cigarette burn in a pillow seemed like a pretty
fair tradeoff. Mother was more engaged and alert than she had
been in years. Even her speech had forward momentum,
mercifully free of those random pauses that leave the listener
in limbo. She was in a state approximating happiness, and who
could begrudge her that.

My release came, as usual, in the guise of the ungodly dinner
hour. The white-coated attendant bore her away, and we all
rode down to the main floor on the elevator. I kissed Mother
goodbye and promised I would call Mildred. As she was wheeled
into the dining room I smiled at the attendant and pushed my
way into the deepening dusk before the old fart with the bad
jokes could nail me again.

I walked home through the park. One of the good features of
living in Westmount is that one can stroll in the parks without
being mugged. At least up to now.

❧

A telephone call before nine a.m. is annoying, before seven a.m.,
alarming. I had fallen into a heavy, early morning sleep, after a
night of insomnia, when I grew dimly aware of a noise on my
night table. After almost dropping the receiver, I wrestled it to
my ear. "Yes?"

"Mr. Chadwick, this is Claire Carswell, manager of Maple
Grove Manor. I'm sorry to have to tell you your mother slipped

away during the night."

I sat up straight. "Where did she go? How did she get out of the building? Have you notified the police?"

"No, no, Mr. Chadwick. What I mean to say is she passed away."

"You mean she died?"

"Yes. I'm so sorry."

"Then why didn't you say so?"

The woman obviously didn't know what to reply, so she said nothing.

"I'll be there as soon as I can, Mrs. Carswell. I'd better call my sister first."

"You do that. We'll look after all the necessary formalities. My sympathy, Mr. Chadwick."

"Thank you. I'll be as quick as possible."

I hung up and headed into the shower. I wanted to be awake when I called Mildred. I wondered if a shot of brandy might help, but decided it was not the best idea on an empty stomach. I turned on the tap and stood, wasting water, as I wasn't in the least dirty. Were I to indulge myself in the solipsistic luxury of guilt I would flagellate myself for not feeling waves of grief over Mother's death. The inescapable fact remained that I was in such a state of emotional fatigue from Elinor's death that all I could register is that a life had ended. That the life in question had been responsible for initiating my own seemed irrelevant; the only moisture on my cheeks came from the showerhead. One cannot fake genuine feeling; at least I can't. Perhaps one day I will be swept with an aching nostalgia for my last remaining parent. What I did feel was an illicit sense of relief that I had outlived Mother and not the other way around. That meant I could see her buried with some dignity. For this I would have to take on my sister, whom I had to call as soon as I finished my shower.

By the time I towelled myself dry, my skin looked not unlike seersucker. I pulled on a robe, fortified myself with a cup of instant microwave coffee, and dialled Mildred's number.

"Mildred, it's Geoffry. An ungodly hour to call, and I apologize."

"Don't tell me. You called to say Mother has been called. I had a dream last night that she had passed away. It jolted me awake, and when I heard the phone ring I just knew."

Ordinarily my inclination is to hang up when the conversation turns to dreams, but in this instance I got lucky.

"It's too early in the day to talk about occult forces, Mildred; but in this instance you are right. The residence director just called to say Mother had 'slipped away' during the night. Dear God, why must people use these arch euphemisms when talking about something as unavoidable as death."

I feared Mildred might weep; she is given to dramatic displays of emotion, but she was so buoyed up by her dire dream and beating me to the draw over Mother's demise that I could tell the eyes above the receiver were dry.

"I shall come down for the funeral of course."

"That's your call, Mildred. There's little point in having

a service as all of Mother's friends have long since died. She wanted to be cremated and buried beside Father. We might have a small ceremony at the gravesite. She also signed an organ donation form, but that was years ago. I seriously doubt her nearly one-hundred-year-old organs will save the race. Besides, I do not want her handled in that undignified manner."

"But if her corneas could enable someone to see ..."

"Then I'll buy that someone a white cane. She must have signed that donor card years ago, when giving bits of oneself away was first fashionable. Bottom line: Father would not have wanted his widow drawn and quartered."

"But, Geoffry ..."

"I am her attorney; I will decide. Now I must dress and get over to Maple Grove to deal with red tape. I'll call you when I get back home. Let's hope they can rustle up a cup of coffee and a muffin."

Sensing that the conversation and the drama were about to end, Mildred lowered her voice. "When I think of poor Mother, all alone ..."

"To die peacefully, in your sleep, at ninety-seven, with never a major illness is not a bad way to go. May we both be so lucky, except for the ninety-seven part. Imagine having lived almost a century; terrifying prospect. I must get over to Maple Grove. I'll call as soon as I have a report."

Death, unlike birth, is a rite of passage hedged around with formalities and rituals. Hacking one's way through these rules and regulations usually involves a certain amount of horse trading. Mother's funeral was a case in point. I had wanted Mother buried with a minimum of fuss. Such had been her expressed wish, and I was more than willing to comply. I arrived at Maple Grove Manor, disgruntled, unshaven, on edge, to find the Director had already begun to execute the necessary formalities. Accustomed to the periodic death of residents, she had an undertaker in her Rolodex. I did not, but it turned out her undertaking firm was the one that had buried Elinor. I had only to request the same coffin that I had chosen for Elinor, and the Director promised to look after the rest.

She had also drafted an obituary notice for the local paper. All I had to do was supply the names of grandchildren, by whom Mother would be sorely missed. I did not include Harold. Funeral private. The Director then suggested, with that self-effacing determination that brooks no opposition, that Mother had been much loved by both residents and staff. Consequently, to deny them the pleasure and diversion of a funeral would be nothing short of mean. A brief ecumenical service could be held in the salon, after which Mother would be taken to the crematorium.

I knew my sister would want some sort of service, one with more emphasis on decorum than dogma. She looks well in black — what woman does not — and she would have the opportunity to play the bereaved daughter. (I know for a fact that she has at least two lace-trimmed handkerchiefs she carries only at funerals.) Since I was overriding her wishes on organ donations, I decided to go along with the service. Once the final prayer had been mumbled, Mother would then be cremated and her ashes buried in the family plot.

This deceptively simple plan took several long distance calls to my sister. Will there be flowers? Yes. Will there be music? No. Will there be a eulogy? If you insist. By the time we had hammered out the details I was too ground down to feel grief. Even Elinor went onto the back burner.

Naturally, Mildred intended to come to Montreal. She would have arrived on a gurney if necessary. I insisted that it was unreasonable for her daughter Catherine to fly all the way from Alberta to be present at the funeral of a woman she had scarcely known. Jennifer was still undergoing a difficult pregnancy, and a pro forma appearance at the service was not worth the risk. We agreed that Richard would accompany his mother in order to represent the third generation.

I did not alert Elinor's children. I doubted they would read the obituary. Most people do not regularly read the death notices until they begin to receive the old age pension. Were I to telephone Jane and Gregory they would feel obliged to come, and for that very reason I did not want them present. Finally, it was done. Tomorrow Mildred and Richard would arrive from Toronto, the small service to take place the following day.

I poured myself a scotch, slid my lamb chops into the oven, and settled down with my *New Yorker* when the telephone rang. My first reaction, as always, was to ignore the goddamn thing. But it could be important, or else something better deal with now.

The display dial showed my sister's number. "Mildred! It's been absolutely hours since we last spoke. How have you managed? What's up?"

"Geoffry," — when my sister puts that particular spin on my name, pitching her voice high on the first syllable and dropping it on the second — I know she is on the hustle. "As you know, Richard and I are driving down tomorrow, but it turns out Harold wants to come along, for the funeral."

"Whatever for? He never knew Mother."

"I know, but she is still part of his family, his real family; and he wants to attend the service. Can he stay with you?"

"I suppose — but why can't he call me himself?"

"He is shy about asking. He feels he has imposed on you too much as it is."

"He's right. But I still want to speak to him. Have him give me a call."

"I will."

About to hang up, I was nailed by another sing-song utterance of my name.

"Geoffry, how long do you think it will take to settle Mother's estate?"

"I can't give you an exact date, but it shouldn't take long. Father left the capital directly to us in trust, the revenue going to Mother for life. Death duties have already been paid. It's just a question of settling outstanding accounts and dividing up the securities. I've already called the accountant. I'll keep you posted."

"Very good. I'll see you tomorrow then."

Mildred rang off, I hoped for the last time today.

# 11

$\mathcal{M}$ildred must have wasted no time in calling Harold, as I was just pouring my second drink when he telephoned.

"Geoffry?"

"Harold, I understand you want to bunk in here again."

"If it wouldn't be too much trouble."

"Harold, listen and listen carefully. There will be trouble — and plenty of it, if you smoke in bed. I specifically asked you not to, and you burned a hole in the pillow."

A brief pause followed. "I told you about that — didn't I?"

"Don't try to con me. You did not mention the hole; further-more, the pillow was underneath three others with the hole on the bottom. And the smell from your visit is finally going away. You will smoke on the balcony off the kitchen, and only there. Otherwise I know a fairly reasonable hotel nearby which has smoking floors. What'll it be?"

"I really would prefer to stay with you, if I may."

"You may, if you agree to my iron-clad rule about smoking. If you have to puff at four p.m. you will drag yourself out of bed and onto the balcony. How is your leg by the way?"

"Healing nicely, thanks. The cast comes off next week."

"You'd better take my room again."

"I really hate to put you out."

"The bathroom is closer, and easier to manage. How long will you be staying?"

"Two nights max. I will drive down tomorrow with Mildred, and she wants to get back the day after the funeral."

"Very good. I'll alert the doorman and leave a key if I have to go out. See you tomorrow."

As I replaced the receiver I resigned myself to two more nights in the guest room. My own bathroom really was more user friendly for someone with a cast. But if I caught him smoking indoors I'd have his head on a plate.

Should I happen to run into Alexander Graham Bell in the hereafter, I shall have some tart things to say. For all its convenience, the telephone is an instrument of the devil; and the following day proved my point time after tiresome time. Although I had carefully put R.S.V.P. Regrets on my invitation to the party for Elinor, any number of people on the guest list, having read Mother's obituary in the morning paper, telephoned to offer condolences. The calls were all so similar I had the distinct impression that I had spent the entire day having one long telephone conversation. They had all read the obituary. A terrible shame really, but she lived an unusually long life. Did she really die peacefully in her sleep, as the obit suggested? One can only hope so. Poor Geoffry. Coming so soon after Elinor's passing. But there you are. However we are so looking forward to the party for Elinor. Will we be there? Wouldn't miss it for the world. What a delightful idea, so much better than a solemn memorial service. We're certain Elinor would have approved. In spite of the sad memory, we're sure it will be loads of fun. We'll toast your mother too. Well, we're thinking of you. Our sympathies, Geoffry dear. Goodbye for now.

Theme with variations. Some wanted to know whether I played bridge, a spare forth always handy to have on the list. I do not play bridge. Others wanted to know whether I wanted to pop down to the Townships for a weekend at the cottage. I did not. One caller wanted to know if I would be interested in meeting an old college friend, now a widow, and thinking seriously of moving back to Montreal. I did not. There were random offers of tickets for the Montreal Symphony, for a rock star appearing at the Bell Centre, for hockey games, none of which I wanted to accept. At the end of the call, almost like a mantra, came the words: "We must have lunch."

("Here lies Geoffry Chadwick. Died peacefully during his afternoon nap from a surfeit of lunch.") As Mother herself would have said, "They mean well." But it is the ones who do not mean well that I applaud. They do not call.

A woman of immense energy, Mildred is fond of announcing

to the world at large that she likes to get up at the crack of dawn. Each time she makes the banal observation I cannot help thinking of the adolescent joke: I was up at the crack of Dawn — and Dawn loved it! Mildred must have jumped out of bed as usual at that ungodly hour and rousted Harold, as it was mid-afternoon when the doorman called to say Mr. Baldwin was on the way up.

I had just awakened from my nap and was making tea, when the doorman rang. Harold limped down the hallway using a cane, considerably more mobile than when he left, but still encumbered by the cast.

"Hello, Geoffry." We shook hands. "Good to see you, even though I have to begin by asking you a favour. The doorman is alone, the porter being sick; and he can't leave his post. Would you mind terribly bringing up my bag. It isn't heavy, but I just can't manage it along with the cane."

"Sure thing. You know your way around. I just made tea. It should be ready when I return."

I rode the elevator with the overnight bag and entered what appeared to be an empty apartment, until I realized Harold had gone out onto the balcony to smoke.

"Mildred won't allow smoking in the car, so I could only smoke when we stopped, for breakfast, for lunch, for coffee, and once to 'rest'."

By now we were seated at the dining room table over mugs of tea. Harold continued. "I do apologize for the pillow; I was sure I had mentioned it. Can I pay for the replacement?"

"No. It wasn't a new one. And pillows die after a while; the bounce goes out of the feathers. So it was time for a new one."

Harold had presented me with not one but two bottles of excellent scotch, so I was somewhat mollified.

"Would you like to lie down for a bit?" I suggested.

"As a matter of fact I would. Mildred wanted to be on the road at the crack of dawn, as she put it, to be out of Toronto before the heavy morning traffic. She had to do all the driving herself as Richard had a last minute crisis. The tenant in the apartment above his managed to block the toilet. Apparently he then went out for the evening, while the appliance continued to overflow. Richard's apartment suffered a lot of water damage, and he decided to stay in Toronto to clean up the mess and deal with the insurance claim. So in order to be ready on time I had to get up early. A short nap would be good."

"Poor Richard. The recurring nightmare of apartment dwellers is what the crackpot, or crackhead in the next apartment might get up to. You go nap, and we'll have tea or a drink when you get up."

While Harold slept I returned calls I had not bothered to answer. Some left their condolences on my voice mail; others, more determined to demonstrate their sympathy, requested I call. By taking the initiative I could head them off at the pass and prevent them from calling again during dinner.

The aforesaid meal was to be simplicity itself: a beefsteak and kidney pie, presently thawing on the kitchen counter, and salad from a bag, the lettuce already shredded. Anybody who wants a gourmet meal in my establishment will have to tune into a cooking show on the telly.

~

It was only after a couple of highballs, made with Harold's Black Label scotch, that the real reason for the visit began to surface. I had decided to mellow out, to use an expression I never use, and enjoy my time with Harold as much as possible. What the hell! A pillow is only a pillow, and I had slain that particular dragon on the telephone. After his nap, Harold limped outside for a cigarette. (No more having a companionable mégot smouldering away in a nearby ash tray when one has to drag a cast outside.) I confess to enjoying my highball with a real person rather than a talking head on the TV news.

Without turning the drinking hour into Twenty Questions, I hoped Harold might volunteer his reason for making a long, tedious drive to attend the funeral of a woman he had never met. I am not from Missouri, but I still found it difficult to believe him, or anyone for that matter, capable of so much family feeling. We no longer lived in the era of saga, when bones of ancestors must be venerated with sacrifice and burnt offerings. Today many of the ancestors live in retirement complexes with daily aerobics, balanced meals, and resident medical care. They are not so much venerated as shunted out of sight. How and why Harold fitted into this generational grid remained to be disclosed.

He shifted position in his chair, pushing his seat against the back and sitting up straight. Having just returned from a cigarette on the kitchen balcony, he took a minute or so to arrange himself, encumbered as he was with a foot in plaster.

"Geoffry, there is no point in beating about the bush. I have a favour to ask."

I too shifted position. "I'm quite prepared to listen."

"To get right to the point, I've been having a few financial problems recently."

"And you want me to lend you money."

"As usual you've beaten me to the draw."

"Before you name a sum, how about a word of explanation. I thought you had been left pretty comfortable, enough to quit working without a worry."

"You are right. But I made some bad decisions: shakey stocks, real estate that did not appreciate, a little gambling."

"Truth time. Are the principal debts gambling debts?"

"Yes, and I am under some pressure to pay up."

"I have to say this: Gambling is a tax on stupidity."

"Don't I know." Harold looked at the floor. "If I pay everything off I won't be able to meet my child support payments. And if I don't, I end up with casts on both legs."

"I see. So the children-slash-grandchildren will take the rap, unless you go to the police. There are laws against extortion."

"The police can only protect me up to a point. If I don't come up with the money I'll have to leave town and drop out of sight."

"I guess it's a bit late for a hand-on-the-shoulder, father-to-son talk on the evils of gambling." I paused for a hefty swallow of my highball. "Okay, Harold, how much do you want?"

Harold shifted slightly, enough to permit him a really deep breath. "You understand it's only a loan."

"I do."

"Could you let me have one hundred thousand dollars?"

"And to think that I heard it on Mulberry Street."

"Excuse me?"

"Oh, nothing. It's just that I was thinking along the lines of a few thousand. One hundred thousand is quite a few thousand."

"I repeat; it's a loan. I'll gladly pay you interest. And I wouldn't ask if I thought you couldn't handle it."

Even as I sat in mute astonishment at the request, I had a sudden flashback of returning to the apartment one morning to find Harold coming out of my office and claiming to be stretching his legs. Had he been going through my desk? So foreign was the idea to me of invading someone else's privacy — Elinor's desk was as inviolate as if locked in a vault — that it never occurred to me Harold might snoop. Added to which I had no doubt that Mildred, in a bout of confessional candour, had blurted out something about Mother's estate now coming to her and me. Harold obviously knew his mark; I could lend him that sum if I wished — which I did not.

Perhaps my suspicion was quite unfounded. Possibly he really had been out "stretching his legs" and wandered without aim into my office. Shit! *En garde*, Geoffry!

I tried my best to appear noncommittal, not easy under the circumstances. "I can only suppose that last observation is speculation on your part. Before we get down to hard bargaining, do you want another drink?"

"Not at the moment, thanks."

"I do."

The pause to pour another highball gave me a moment to reflect. I do not bargain well, not having been raised to. As a tourist I always pay the price asked, often to the astonishment of the street vendor. I find bargaining strictly infra dig. If I can't pay the asking price I'll do without. Elinor agreed with me, often walking away from something she wanted because, once having ascertained the lowest price would go still lower were she to turn her back, she felt demeaned. And bugger their cultural sensitivities.

I carried my drink back into the TV alcove, fully prepared to haggle. And with my own son? What hath God wrought?

"Harold, let me ask you one question. If, as you claim, you are so strapped for cash you are asking me for a large loan, how do you propose to pay me back?"

Harold's broad forehead creased briefly; then, as if attempting to erase any visible sign of anxiety, he managed to smile. "I have some long term investments, bonds mostly, on which I will lose considerably should I redeem them now. I also have a house in a part of Toronto on the verge of gentrification. I shall go back to work, live frugally. I'll manage."

Harold made it all sound as though he were about to embark

on the latest fad diet, not place himself in debt for a large sum of money. If he really was up against the wall, he managed not to let it show.

"You have asked me for one hundred thousand. How much of that will go to pay debts?"

Harold thought for a moment. "Just about all of it."

"Do you have any paperwork I might see?"

"Not with me."

"I see. Which is to say, I don't. Look, Harold, I don't know what you think I am worth, but for me one hundred thousand is a great deal of money. I cannot believe you expect me to hand it over simply because you have said please."

Harold's pose of good natured bonhomie began to develop cracks. "It's not the least bit cold outside. Will you come with me while I smoke?"

"Sure thing. I'll bring your glass."

I held the balcony door open for Harold, then followed him outside. The view, unprepossessing and inoffensive, was of small yards and a lane. Harold lost no time in lighting up and inhaling right down to his knees. I should not have made the next remark. The Devil made me do it. "If you keep on puffing away at those things you won't live long enough to pay off any debts."

Harold, who had been supporting himself on the balcony rail, turned around, so abruptly in fact that he stumbled. I reached out to steady him, but he regained balance.

"Goddammit, Geoffry, do you have to take advantage of my

cap-in-hand situation to deliver platitudes on smoking. As if I haven't heard them all."

I laughed out loud. "Fuck you too, O son and heir. Now why don't you stop bullshitting your dear old dad and tell me exactly how much you really need."

Harold had the good grace to smile, rather a forced smile I have to admit, but a modified rictus nonetheless. "Sixty thousand."

"That's more like it. Finish your cigarette while I check on our dinner. I would like a little time to think. Perhaps we should speak of other things for the remainder of the evening. There is a movie at nine p.m. I would like to watch."

"What time is the service tomorrow?"

"Ten a.m. That's when the residents are at their most alert. Also it means that Mildred can get started on the drive back to Toronto by noon."

I went into the kitchen to escape further talk. I needed some time to absorb what Harold had proposed. Also I wanted him to sweat a little. Already a plan was taking shape; but, like green tomatoes, it had to ripen.

∽

The funeral service for Mother turned out to be considerably less dreadful than that for Elinor, mainly because there was no music. Nothing destroys a ceremony, festive or solemn, more quickly than badly played music. The upright piano sat, silent and unplayed, in its corner of the beige and green lounge. Also, in deference to the age and limited attention span of the residents, the occasion was short. Mildred had gone into a huddle with the ad hoc minister in order to feed him enough information for a brief eulogy. The little talk held few surprises: long and distinguished life, will be sorely missed by her children and grandchildren, a woman of great character and probity, in her day a pillar of the community, a vibrant presence at Maple Grove Manor, where she will also be sorely missed. Let us pray.

One or two of the residents nodded off. Three or four wept a few tears. Flanked by Harold and me, austere and stylish in black, Mildred wept on cue. I put a navy blue arm around her shoulders. Were I to have shed a tear I fear it would have been for Elinor. Considering that the funeral was for my own mother, I thought that to weep for someone else would not be quite fair. My eyes remained dry.

Harold stared impassively ahead. He had managed a blazer and dark tie, somewhat undermined by tan chinos, whose wide legs pulled on over the cast. Whatever his thoughts, I doubt they rested on the woman in the coffin, firmly closed in spite of Mildred's objections. I had not yet told him what I intended to do about the loan. As he and Mildred were to leave for Toronto as soon as we had visited the crematorium, he no doubt felt more than mild curiosity about my decision.

Most nights I lie awake, sleep just tantalizingly out of reach, and replay episodes of my life with Elinor. Last night I had other concerns. The onset of old age may have made me just a bit hard of hearing, but I am not hard of thinking. It would not have taken a stratospheric I.Q. to realize Harold had a serious purpose in looking me up. Well and good. Most people in this ungenerous world have what is currently called an agenda, so why not my son. In another time, another place, I might have been dismayed by the naked self-interest in Harold's courting me. If only; isn't life made up of a series of "if onlys." But if only Harold had taken the time to become my friend on top of being my biological son, what might I have not done for him.

To begin with, had he turned out to be less self-serving he may well have found his way into my will, and for considerably more than one hundred thousand dollars. But he had played his cards fast and recklessly. I intended to lend him the money, reasonably certain that I probably would not see either Harold or the money again.

At four a.m. my regret was deeper than I cared to admit, even to myself. I replayed the last forty-eight hours before Harold had returned to Toronto, when I honestly believed I had discovered a son and, more important, a friend. It was a kind of honeymoon, innocent of passion, but flooded with happiness. In a perverse kind of way I was fortunate that the recent death of Elinor, and now that of Mother, had blunted my responses. I was drugged by death. Perhaps one day I would grieve over the son who came into my life only to see me as a cash cow. In the meantime, screw the manipulative little bastard. At the moment I had more important things to regret.

Reality intruded in the guise of four blue-suited men from the undertaker's moving quietly to wheel the coffin out to the hearse. Steeling myself to face, once again, the sight of someone I had loved sliding down rollers into a furnace, I put Harold out of my thoughts. Besides, Mildred needed an arm. Suddenly it seemed as if she had truly realized that it was in effect her own mother who lay in the coffin. This time her tears sprang from genuine grief, and I steered her out of the building and into the limousine.

∽

After the brief ceremony, Harold and I stood outside the crematorium. To the north, the foothills of the Laurentian Mountains stood as indistinct shapes, blurred as they were by the amber autumn haze.

"Harold, to the point. You asked me for one hundred thousand dollars. You admitted that you need sixty thousand. I will split the difference and lend you eighty thousand. That will enable you to pay your debts and give you something to live on until you find your feet. You understand this is a loan. I believe that as you are both my son and a gentleman no paperwork is necessary. Let us shake hands, and the deal is done."

Harold shook my proffered hand. "What can I say but thanks."

"That will do nicely for the moment. It will take me three or four days to raise the money, which I will have transferred to your bank in Toronto. You can leave the necessary information on my voice mail."

"Here comes Mildred."

For once my sister was not playing at grief for an audience. Mother's death had affected her more than I would have thought possible. To die quietly while asleep after almost a century of living is hardly the stuff of tragedy, but death always has a curious effect on the living. Mildred embraced me. As we have never been a touchy-feely kind of family, the unaccustomed gesture suggested Mildred was "not herself," as Mother might have said.

"I'm sorry I have to get back to Toronto; one of those engagements I couldn't postpone. But I'll be down next week for the party."

"Plan to stay an extra day. I'll arrange for Mother's ashes to be buried in the family plot beside Father. We can both be there. And you can help me to clear out Mother's room."

Mildred managed a smile. "That would be ideal. I'm not going to say 'Poor Mother' because she is at peace. What I really want to say is 'Poor me,' and that would be maudlin. Well, Harold, are you ready to head out?"

"Whenever you say."

I embraced Mildred, shook hands with Harold, and they drove away. The limousine drove me home. And that was that.

Were I to avoid stepping on cracks in the sidewalk, taking the last sandwich on a plate, reusing stamps that have not been franked, putting aluminum cans into the garbage, or tossing begging letters into the wastebasket unopened, could I reasonably hope that the Great Father in the Sky might hold back on funerals for a while? Perhaps I should light a candle in church, but is there a surcharge if you are not Catholic? A burnt offering could all too easily pass as a cooking experiment gone amiss; and even if I could find a virgin to sacrifice, I would be in contravention of the criminal code.

I compromised on a couple of Bloody Marys and an omelette at the Lord Elgin Club. The young and probably available waiter had the nicest bubble butt I have seen in a long time, and for a few moments I allowed fantasies of the living to banish solemn thoughts of the dead. I know Elinor would have approved.

Standing outside the Lord Elgin Club waiting for the cab I had ordered, I was ambushed by Angela MacKay: good tweed suit, matching handbag and shoes, gloves, hat, pearls, and her valiant air of resisting age. I had not seen her since before Elinor's illness. Angela used to court me during the days when I was a hostess's delight, a single man who had once been married. ("Thank goodness Geoffry isn't — well, you know.") However I was firm in resisting her blandishments of white wine, brie, and chamber music. After a while she ran out of steam, much to my relief.

"Well, well, Geoffry. Long time no see. Still so handsome."

A wide gap separates "handsome" from "still handsome," but I was in no mood to quibble.

"Angela! Good to see you. I've just called a cab. Can I drop you anywhere?"

"No thanks, I'm just on my way to see my doctor — in the next block."

"Nothing serious, I hope."

"No, no, just the annual checkup." She smiled her bullet-proof smile. "I understand you're taking over the club for a party. My husband has just joined the board of directors, so I know absolutely everything. Is it for your birthday?"

"No, it's not." I did not elaborate. She was trolling for an invitation, so I played dumb.

"That must be a relief for your friends," she continued. "After all, what do you give the man who has everything?"

"I'd say penicillin or the last rites."

After a couple of uncertain seconds Angela laughed her social stage laugh, descending "ha's" in intervals of a third. "Oh, Geoffry, you're so droll."

Over the years I had accepted Angela's hospitality from time to time. Perhaps the opportunity had come for a *quid pro quo*, and she evidently wanted to attend my soiree. "The party is for Elinor, sort of a belated wake. If you and Stephen are able to come I'd be delighted."

"That would be lovely, Geoffry. We were visiting Stephen's family in Victoria when Elinor died, and we couldn't attend the funeral service."

Taking a small morocco-bound diary from her impeccably understated handbag, Angela jotted down the particulars. On one hand I thought it perhaps a bit tacky to use Elinor's memorial party to pay off social debts; on the other Angela had indicated she knew about the funeral. Elinor would have given her the benefit of the doubt, not to mention that my Bloody Marys, plus a carafe of wine, had mellowed me out. Also, my nap beckoned.

Angela had not mentioned seeing Mother's funeral notice, and I did not bring the subject up.

Further chitchat was made unnecessary by the arrival of my cab.

"Well, Angela, off you go to the medicine man. Does he have plants?"

"Plants? I don't really know."

"You'd better check. Elinor always said to avoid a doctor whose plants are dead. See you at the party."

I scrambled into the cab and drove away, leaving Angela uncertain about the intended joke. Angela either has selective hearing, or is a little slow on the uptake, perhaps both. I once told her I had a rock garden but the rocks died.

"What a shame!" she had replied, without the trace of a smile. When I come back in another life I hope it won't be as a stand-up comic.

༄

The following morning early found me calling my financial advisor for suggestions on how best to raise the money I was lending to Harold. A dour, Scottish-Canadian, Hamish Maclean believes strongly in all the Presbyterian sins, of which perhaps the most egregious is to spend capital. Had I been dying from an affliction at once obscure and probably terminal from which only a hugely expensive operation might rescue me, he would have given it the green light only if it could be paid for from income. At times he behaves as though my money were not really my money at all but merely a monthly allowance which he is kind enough to permit me.

Considering the sum involved, I thought it best to confront him in person. His secretary is one of those staunch spinsters who would gladly walk on hot coals for her employer. I once suspected she might be in love with Hamish; but if she were, the passion would have been based less on physical chemistry than a shared goal to foil spending on the part of their clients. I know she thought me frivolous for marrying late in life, and furthermore for a second time, wives being an expensive luxury. Hamish bestowed begrudging congratulations, as he knew Elinor to be woman of independent means.

I called his office. "Good morning, Miss Gladwell, it is Geoffry Chadwick speaking. I would like to see Hamish today."

I could sense her bristling on the other end. "Goodness me, Mr. Chadwick, you should have given me some warning. Mr. Maclean is a very busy man. He doesn't have any free time today."

Before Elinor died I would have played along, cajoling, agreeing hers was a tough row to hoe, throwing myself on her good nature, and, finally, graciously, being granted an audience as if with the Pope.

That was then. "Miss Gladwell, it is important that I see Mr. Maclean, preferably this morning. I am not asking for an appointment; I am telling you I wish to see Hamish before the stock markets close for the day. You are his secretary ..."

"Please, Mr. Chadwick, Executive Assistant!"

"Yes, yes, whatever. Eleven a.m. would suit me just fine. And I don't care if you have to bump the Prime Minister, the Governor General, and the President United States of America. Just do it."

Before she had a chance to remonstrate I hung up.

Hamish Maclean has his ear to the ground. He reads the obituary column the way other men read the sports pages or racing forms. By now he knew that Constance Chadwick had died and that her son would be coming into a nice little inheritance, meaning his management fee would increase accordingly. Consequently, at eleven a.m. I was ushered into the office of Hamish Maclean, past the steel-rimmed glare of Gladwell, as her employer called her. The office itself left little doubt as to the owner's sympathies. From the large painting of Highland cattle behind the desk, past the furniture upholstered in one of the uglier tartans, to the pen and pencil stand featuring a large cairngorm, the visitor was transported to a garage sale version of Bonnie Scotland.

Hamish had been raised in Southern Ontario; his flat vowels offered no hint of the Highlands. After shaking his dry hand and being gestured towards one of the plaid chairs, I faced him across an expanse of desk, intimidating for its complete lack of clutter.

"Well, Geoffry, sorry to hear about your mother." I smiled in acknowledgment of his warm expression of sympathy. "Now, what can I do for you?"

"Hamish, I'm lending my son eighty thousand dollars, cash;

and I want your advice on the best way to raise it."

Monochromatic faces do not ordinarily change colour, but a faint flush spread across the sand-coloured features facing me. "I didn't know you had a son."

"Neither did I until only recently. But there he is, life size and living colour. Furthermore, he is in a jam and he needs the money."

Now all business, Hamish folded his hands and nailed me with a hard, uncompromising stare. "What is he offering in the way of security?"

"A handshake. I know you don't find that very reassuring, but if he had any real security he wouldn't need the money. Look, Hamish, I know what you are thinking, and I could script the admonitory speech you are about to make. Now I know I muscled my way in here, past the Gorgon Medusa, and that your schedule is tight; so let's cut to the chase. I want eighty thousand dollars. What is the most expedient way to raise it?"

I too can be intimidating; furthermore, even seated, I am considerably taller than Hamish. Wisely deciding to forego the pleasures of disapproval, he opened a drawer and took out my file. In a matter of minutes I had instructions on what to sell and why. Hamish knows his business, which is why I have put up for years with his dour disapproval. Having obtained what I came for, I decided to leave on a positive note.

"What I will inherit from Mother's estate will more than plug the hole in my portfolio occasioned by the loan. I will be in touch when my sister and I get down to sharing the spoils.

In the meantime, I won't take up any more of your time."

We shook hands awkwardly across the broad expanse of desk. As I left the office, Miss Gladwell managed a curt nod. I was, after all, a client of long standing. On the way back to my apartment I stopped in at a florist and sent her a dozen white roses with a note of thanks for getting me in to see Hamish on such short notice. There was not an ounce of gratitude in my gesture. Rather, I wanted to put her on the defensive, so the next time I wanted a favour she would be obliged to comply, and without the *pro forma* disapproval.

༄

Three days later, I had the money in place and ready to transfer to Harold's account in Toronto. I will not say I had mixed feelings. When someone says he has "mixed feelings" about a situation it usually means the course of action he is obliged to take is the last one he would voluntarily choose. In my case I had no desire to relinquish a large sum of money to Harold, but I had given my word. In spite of handshakes and positive thinking, I understood that the chances of seeing my money again were close to zero. If there was a plus side, I was freed from any future requests my son might make. All the money would find its way back into the economy and goose the GNP. I was not about to go hungry as a result of the loan; furthermore, had I known about Harold earlier in my life the chances are he would have cost me much more over the years than the amount I was about to unload.

None of these specious, feel-good arguments served to mitigate the intense reluctance I felt about dispatching the cash. How I wished Elinor were here to act as a kind of sentient sounding board. Over a highball or two she would have heard me out and then offered advice, usually sound. In this instance I am, like Ivory Flakes, 99 & 44/100s per cent certain that she would have come down on the side of family obligation, regardless of how financially unsound the transaction. For better or for worse, Harold was my son. I would be perfectly within my rational rights to discount this latecoming and slender tie. Many men have inadvertently fertilized an egg without subsequently incurring a large financial obligation. But — a very large but — a dicey roll of the dice made me the progenitor of a man who risked having his legs broken for nonpayment of debts. I understood clearly onto which side of the argument Elinor would have moved. If only she were here to tell me herself.

She might even have said something about a clear conscience. In my experience, a clear conscience all too often means a defective memory, and after almost seventy years any conscience has taken quite a number of hits. Mine certainly had, God only knows, and perhaps still would. But not today.

I reached for the telephone. "Harold, it's Geoffry. I have the money ready, and it will be transferred to your account today. It is convenient that we both use the same bank. So there you are."

"You know, Geoffry, I am not an inarticulate man. English teacher and all of that. But words really do fail. To admit that I am grateful falls so far short of the mark that I am ashamed.

What can I say other than that I will repay you as soon as I possibly can."

"That last statement has a more welcome ring than the professions of thanks. Pay me whenever you can. Oh, and consider the loan interest free. Are you coming down for my party?"

"I'm not sure at the moment. Mildred has offered me a lift; but the cast comes off tomorrow and I'll have to discover how mobile I am."

"There are plenty of chairs at the club, and I'll make sure the staff keeps you well supplied with food and drink. The one hitch is that I've already offered the spare room to a friend."

"Not to worry. Mildred's friend, the one she stays with, has offered me her son's room. He's in the U.K. for a year on scholarship, so lodging is not a problem."

"Well then, come if you can."

"I will. Well, so long, and thanks. As they say, 'You're the greatest thing since sliced bread.'"

"What do you suppose was the greatest thing before sliced bread? Stay in touch."

As I replaced the receiver I had the oddest sensation, almost a premonition, as if I had just said goodbye, not to the phone conversation but to Harold himself. He had come into my life via the telephone. Was he to exit the same way? Not having an answer I sought refuge in a Bloody Mary. How often have I read that drinking alone, and furthermore at noon, is the first step on the downward slippery slope. Maybe it was, but — Jesus H. Christ — did it ever taste good.

# 12

The few remaining days prior to the party passed in a welter of trivia. I had to take any number of calls from guests who had changed their plans and couldn't come for one reason or another. The drama of Agamemnon being murdered in his bath or of Oedipus discovering his true parentage was as nothing compared with the breast beating over not being able to attend Elinor's party. Hyperbole ran rampant over the telephone wires as one after another female voice declared itself "absolutely devastated" not to be coming. It did not escape my notice that none of the men invited had telephoned last minute cancellations. An open bar is a huge magnet, and the prospect of a free drunk heals all but the most dire ailments. One woman telephoned and asked if she could bring her houseguests: her sister, brother-in-law, and their three children. I said no; it was a wake, not a rally. She hung up in a huff.

I telephoned the Lord Elgin Club with a final head count, about one hundred and eighty, give or take a few. I took the suit I intended to wear to the tailor for pressing. The garment really did not need the iron, but I did it for Elinor. I purchased a new tie in royal blue and hunter green stripes, two of Elinor's favourite colours. I would wear a shirt with French cuffs — how they do get in the way — that allowed me to wear cufflinks Elinor gave me, oval gold discs with my monogram. Probably the last time I would wear them. All in all I was prepared to be "The grandest tiger in the jungle," just like the ones who stole clothes from Little Black Sambo in the children's classic now banned on grounds of political incorrectness. If the tale had to be censored the cause should have been for bad geography. Little Black Sambo is obviously African, but tigers are found in India. I was even prepared to shoehorn my ageing feet into thin-soled oxfords. It has been suggested that fashion is a hobby for those who wish they had talent, but I wanted to look my best for Elinor.

Desmond telephoned to say he would like to accept my offer of a room and an invitation to the party. He would also like to spend the following day in the McGill Library, returning to Toronto on Sunday. I was pleased he had decided to visit. There is always a let-down after a party, especially if one is host; and having Desmond here would give me someone with whom to have a post mortem. Discussing a party in the wee hours can be almost more entertaining than the party itself, and I felt something very like relief that I would not have to face the shank of the evening alone.

My sister telephoned just as I was pouring my first drink of the evening.

"Mildred, don't tell me you've called to say you're not coming down for the party."

"Not at all. But it is still about the party that I called. I've decided to take the train. It gets into Montreal mid-afternoon, and I can scoot over to Lillian's, change, and take a cab to the Lord Elgin. I had originally intended to drive, but I really dislike the 401. It's both dangerous and boring, and I don't want to arrive at the party a complete wreck."

To hear Mildred admit to human weakness was not unlike hearing the Delphic Sybil uttering smut. It went against the accepted order, and in Mildred's case served as yet another reminder that we were all growing older.

"I think you're showing great common sense," I said. "I wouldn't drive to Toronto for all the tea in China. How much tea is there in China, by the way?"

"I have no idea. But to discuss Chinese tea is not why I called. I had offered Harold a ride to Montreal, if he wanted to come along. I feel awful about backing out, but I do find that drive absolutely exhausting."

"You get no argument from me. I wouldn't drive to Toronto for all the tea in India."

"Geoffry, do be serious for a moment. I telephoned Harold to beg off — and to suggest he join me on the train, if he so wished, only to be informed — by one of those irritating recorded voices — that his number was no longer in service.

I dialled again, with the same result. Then I called the operator who tried the number and told me the same thing. Harold's phone has been disconnected. Have you any idea how I can reach him?"

"I'm afraid, not, Mildred. I spoke with him only a few days ago, and it was business as usual."

"Wasn't he staying with a friend for a while?"

"Yes, he was. I have the number here somewhere." I dug out my phone directory. "Do you want to give him a try, or shall I?"

Ever officious, Mildred said she would call and report back to me. More than happy to let her do the telephoning, I said I intended to be at home for the rest of the evening. And when Mildred called back within the hour to say that the friend had no idea that Harold's phone had been cut off or how Harold could be reached, I was not in the least surprised. "Take the money and run" has become a standard tag line, but Harold had taken the advice to the letter. He had taken the money and disappeared.

৵

Three drinks later, two more than I generally have in the evening, I had more or less come to terms with the idea that Harold had pocketed the money I sent and dropped out of sight. Where did not matter. He had vanished, and so had the cash. I could, just possibly, be mistaken; but a "little voice," in this instance shrill and raucous, told me I had seen the last of Harold and the eighty thousand.

How I would have liked to run the situation past Elinor, over a couple of drinks, although I already knew what she would have said. He was my son. He needed the money, or claimed he did; as I had no way of disproving his claim, I really had no choice. She would probably have gone on to say that my responsibility towards him had been more than fulfilled, and there would be no question of even a token legacy in my will. Then, in conclusion, she might have said something along the lines of "It's only money, and neither of us is going to starve." She might even have tipped me a broad wink and suggested I was worth one hell of a lot more than eighty thousand on the open market, even slightly used. We would have laughed, shrugged, sent out for pizza, and watched a movie. Now that these commonplace evenings are over, I feel like an exile. Possibly a couple of drinks, pizza all dressed, and a 1940's movie is not everyone's idea of paradise; but in my case it came close — and how much more in retrospect.

Now I must eat something. Then, like Samuel Pepys, "And so to bed."

๛

The day of the party shimmered with the haze of late autumn, a screen almost like mist. We basked in what seemed like a second Indian summer. Desmond and I stood on the sidewalk outside my building waiting for the taxi to take us to the Lord Elgin Club. If I say so myself, I looked very dapper, the well-cut blue suit helping to conceal the unkinder effects of gravity.

Elinor's cufflinks gave off a dull gleam in the smokey sunlight. As usual, Desmond was preppy perfect in tattersall and one of my ties — beige and cocoa stripes — which we both agreed went better with Le Look than the one he had packed.

The taxi pulled up and we climbed in, Desmond with more agility than I. Sensing that we both faced a social marathon, he tactfully refrained from small talk, respecting the temporary calm before the storm. I had not slept very much the previous night; I was so pumped with adrenalin I could have run a marathon. A number of conclusions had been reached between brief moments of dozing off, and as the taxi made its leisurely way along Sherbrooke Street — we were caught up in what is whimsically called rush hour traffic — I went over them again.

The first and most important was that tonight we were all going to say goodbye to Elinor for the last time. This went for me as well. Tomorrow I must begin to move on, to live out the rest of my life without allowing grief to degenerate into self-indulgence. Already I had begun to let go, which is to say I was beginning to remember my life with Elinor without a pang of dismay. It has been said that the passage of time heals emotional wounds just as it does to those of the body. I have not found this to be true. Time does not heal; it anesthetizes, dulling the pain rather than making it disappear. I would never get over Elinor's death, but I would accommodate myself to the void. And far more terrifying than coming to grips with life without Elinor is the idea that we might never have met, that I would not have lived those brief but wonderful years in her company. Or, to

borrow lines from Tennyson: "'Tis better to have loved and lost/
Than never to have loved at all."

About my mother's death I was more serene. She had lived
her life and was sitting and sipping and waiting to die. Perhaps
that makes me sound unfeeling, but North American society
lives in denial of death. Old age is infantilized with geriatrics in
track suits and ghastly birthday parties where the confection-
er's cake reads Ninety Years Young. But once my father died,
Mother drifted happily into old age, helped along by alcohol
and a strong constitution, which helped her to metabolize it.
The stark truth remains that she was my mother, my real mother,
not my adoptive, foster, surrogate, birth, step, or den. Real
mothers are unique, only one per person; and with the death of
a parent a door shuts. I wonder whether I won't miss the idea
of a mother rather than the woman herself. I won't regret the
visits to Maple Grove Manor, the nasty old man in the lobby
and his appalling jokes, Mother's overheated room, a warmish
vodka and water, and conversation like unmatched beads on a
knotted string. Yet it is an odd sensation to be an orphan at seventy,
a bit past the age for Dickensian pathos. Were Elinor to be still
alive I would doubtless be feeling Mother's death more keenly,
but there are limits as to how much grief one can honestly feel.
And Mother herself, the least assertive of women, would have
considered excessive displays of grief, or anything else, in the
worst possible taste. I am her son after all, so I do the best I can.

Harold appears to have dropped out of my life. He had obtained what he sought and vanished down the Memory Hole.

Whether or not he needed the money to pay off ominous debts, or whether the whole thing was a scam no longer really mattered. For a brief time I had thoroughly enjoyed his company, our shared laughter, and the sheer novelty of discovering a son. Also, were I given to bouts of macho vanity, he had convinced me that during my stud-muffin days I was not shooting blanks. However, our encounter had been too brief to make a lasting impression. My own father always maintained you had to earn the respect and affection of your family; the mere accident of relationship by blood does not necessarily guarantee a place of honour.

In the smaller hours of the morning it occurred to me that had Harold really dropped out of sight then so had his child support payments. I must call Barbara and find out where she stood financially. I had liked her, and now with time on my hands I would return to Toronto and meet my grandchildren. I wanted to size them up for myself and disregard Harold's jaundiced estimation of his own children. It is not in my nature to be a loveable old codger grandad, like a figure from a Norman Rockwell *Saturday Evening Post* cover, but I could certainly rise to birthday presents and perhaps a visit to New York City. While in Toronto I would stay with Mildred, not that I wouldn't be happier and more comfortable in a hotel; but I know she prefers me to stay under her roof, sacred claims of family and the rest of that cant. To be fair to Mildred, she is an excellent cook; she buys only the best ingredients and cooks them with a tact she fails to demonstrate with people.

One dines well at Chez Mildred, and now that I am reduced once again to cooking for myself the prospect of good meals is a blandishment. People are said to mellow with age. I wish Mildred would stop stalling and begin the mellowing process, but this too may come to pass.

While visiting Mildred I could go out for dinner one night with my new friend Desmond, an evening off for good behaviour as it were. I have never made friends, close friends, easily; and at seventy one has one's friends, just the way Boston matrons are said to have their hats. But I really liked Desmond, and to have made a new friend at my age is most welcome. Who knows. Now that Larry is on the wagon for life he and Desmond might pick up where they left off, once Larry has made the discovery that moving aimlessly from city to city solves nothing; and that to be constantly in motion is no substitute for a productive life. All this lay in the future, or "down the road" in today's newspeak.

By now the traffic had opened up enough to allow our taxi past the Roddick Gates opening onto the McGill campus. Soon we would reach our destination. My immediate concern was to get through the party. After that came the tomorrows, somewhat foreshortened at seventy; but with Mother's genes I might well hang in for a while yet. As the taxi pulled up in front of the columns flanking the Lord Elgin Club I could almost believe I saw a light at the end of the tunnel. Let's hope it isn't a train.

Desmond beat me to the draw in paying for the cab, and we climbed out onto the sidewalk.

"Well, kiddo," I said. "This is it."

We went inside.